DEAR ARC READER

THIS IS AN UNCORRECTED PROOF
NOT FOR SALE OR DISTRIBUTION

Thank you for reading and reviewing this Advanced Reader Copy.

This is an uncorrected proof. The final version may contain some changes.

LOVE EVERLASTING

including

THE YOUNGERS

Then Came You

Taking a Chance on Love

All I Want Is You

My One and Only

THE THORNTONS

The Nearness of You

The Very Thought of You

If I Can't Have You

Dream a Little Dream of Me

Someone to Watch Over Me

Till There Was You

I'll Be Home for Christmas

THE PRINCE I LOVE TO HATE

THE HEIR AFFAIR DUET

IRIS MORLAND

BLUE VIOLET PRESS LLC

The Prince I Love to Hate
Copyright © 2021 by Iris Morland
Published by Blue Violet Press LLC
Seattle, Washington

Cover design by Qamber Designs

THE PRINCE I LOVE
TO HATE

CHAPTER ONE

"You have got to be kidding me," I said as the taxi driver stopped in front of the house.

No, it wasn't a house. It was a mansion. More accurately, it was an entire *estate*.

The driver gave me a strange look. "You touring this place?"

"Yeah, kinda." I handed him a few Euros and opened the car door, rather wishing I could ask him to go with me. But he'd already driven off by the time I'd been tempted to turn around and ask him to tour the place with me.

Okay, *tour* wasn't the right word. *Wrap my head around what I was seeing* would be more accurate.

I mean, I'd known that Grandda Gallagher had been rich—he'd left me a rather large inheritance, after all—but *this* rich? I'd somehow missed that memo.

"He probably buried gold bars in the backyard," my older brother Liam had said darkly before I'd flown from Seattle all the way to Ireland. "Along with all of the bodies."

As far as I knew, our grandda hadn't been a murderer—just a judgmental arsehole, as Liam liked to call him. Or when Liam was feeling polite, he called Grandda by the moniker Old Man Gallagher. Liam never called him Grandda or Grandfather or Grandpa. Liam had hated our grandda for how he'd treated our mam, and even when he'd died, Liam hadn't forgiven him.

I swallowed, my throat dry. Why had I wanted to come to Dublin again? I should've stayed in Seattle making lattes for tech nerds with terrible social skills. Having some guy named Chad get passive aggressive with me because I'd forgotten to leave room in his Americano for cream would be preferable to whatever it was I was doing now.

The ocean behind me was the only noise besides my heart pounding in my ears. There were stairs down to the harbor; above, stairs to the house. Or mansion. Was that a fucking *turret?* Geez, this was straight out of a fairy tale.

When a real life, actual butler answered the door, I almost started laughing. Instead, I wished that I'd changed out of my ratty t-shirt and even rattier sneakers at the airport. The only person who I thought would be here was Grandda's lawyer, Mr. McDonnell.

"Um," I said, as the butler stared down his nose at me. "I'm Niamh Gallagher."

The butler didn't even blink, but his lip curled ever so slightly, most likely from hearing my flat, American accent. "Right this way, miss," he said blandly. As he turned, I was surprised I didn't hear creaking noises, like a mannequin being repositioned in a store window.

The butler led me upstairs to what could only be described as a parlor. Or was it a sitting room?

The room itself faced the ocean, and I was drawn to the large bay windows. I could smell the sea salt in the air, the windows wide open and curtains dancing lightly in the breeze.

A telescope sat nearby, and I couldn't help but lean down and peer into it. I could make out some boats in the water, along with some gulls circling. One dove into the water and came up with a wiggling fish.

As I was waiting for Grandda's lawyer, Mr. McDonnell, to arrive, I began to explore the room: with the white walls and the similarly white and oak furniture, I had a feeling no one ever ate anything like lasagna in this place.

I wondered if Grandda had decorated this place himself, but given what Liam had always told me about him, I doubted it. He'd seemed too focused on controlling Liam and me from afar, or earning gobs of money, to care what kind of furniture was in his palatial mansion.

I looked at my phone. Had the butler forgotten to tell Mr. McDonnell I was here? Maybe the butler hadn't been oiled enough this morning and had frozen in place as he'd gone in search of this mysterious lawyer, like the Tin Man in *The Wizard of Oz*.

I poked my head out of the sitting room: the hallway was deserted. Well, I was the previous owner's granddaughter, and currently no one technically lived here, so I could explore without getting in trouble, right?

I began to wander, taking in the view of the ocean from various windows, enjoying the artwork on the walls. Liam, a photographer, would certainly enjoy the various collections of photographs in this place.

As I rounded the corner in the opposite direction from where I'd come with the butler, I found a door that led to an outdoor terrace that was filled with a variety of potted plants. It was a beautifully sunny day, and I shaded my eyes against the bright sunlight.

When Mr. McDonnell had sent me that infamous letter asking me to come to Dublin for some business regarding Grandda's estate, I hadn't thought much of it. Grandda had died five years ago, leaving me a sizable inheritance that had paid for my college tuition at Harvard the following fall.

Liam, having fallen out with Grandda ages ago, had gotten only a small amount of money when he'd turned eighteen many years ago. So it had made sense that I would inherit anything else. I'd initially balked at having to travel so far just to sign a few papers, though. Email was a thing in Ireland, too.

It was when Mr. McDonnell had informed me that he had information on the whereabouts of my da, Connor Gallagher, that I'd changed my mind.

Da had run out on me, Liam, and our mam before I'd even been born. I'd never known him. As far as Liam was concerned, he was dead to us, and that was that. (Liam really liked to hold grudges against the men in our family.)

But I'd always wanted to know more about Da: why he'd left, if he was even still alive. It had been something that had niggled at me for years. When Mr. McDonnell's letter had landed in my mailbox, it had felt like destiny.

I heard someone swear, breaking through my

reverie. Rounding the corner, I found a man holding his thumb to his mouth.

In the sunlight, all I could make out was that he was young and had what could only be described as *golden* hair. It literally sparkled in the light. When he turned his face toward me, I nearly choked on my own spit.

He was *ridiculously* good-looking; there was no other way to describe it. Lean, chiseled jaw; tanned skin; golden hair; tall, muscular, but not bulky. He had that perfect, symmetrical face that was either the result of amazing genetics or a very talented plastic surgeon.

I was leaning against some kind of fruit tree, too enthralled by this golden man to notice that I was leaning too much of my weight on the tree. A branch snapped, and Golden Man swiveled his head in my direction to see me staring like an idiot.

"Good morning," he said to me, surprisingly calm given the whole staring thing. "Why are you hiding in a fruit tree?" A pause, then he added, "Miss?"

I pushed away from the tree, blushing harder when the broken branch fell to the ground. Mortified, I picked it up, like I could somehow put it back onto the tree. I eventually just dropped into the pot and hoped I hadn't completely ruined the poor plant.

Golden Man clucked his tongue at me. "You'll have to pay for that, you know. Do you know how expensive these trees are?"

His accent was definitely not Irish, or English for that matter. It sounded closest to a French accent. As my brain took in that interesting fact, he'd gotten closer to me. I could then make out that he had lovely gray eyes.

Of course he did, I thought in annoyance. Nothing

banal like brown eyes for this golden man. He probably never farted or got pimples, either.

"Um," was all I could manage. Why was I acting like a thirteen-year-old girl at a One Direction concert? I fixed cars for fun and had been around all kinds of men at my local car shop. They were men who'd try their best either to rile me or get into my pants, often both.

But I was already out of sorts in a country I'd never really known, at a place I hadn't known existed, and apparently that was enough to render me tongue-tied.

Golden Man was peering at me expectantly, a similarly golden eyebrow raised in question. "Who are you, miss?" he said finally.

"I'm Niamh Gallagher."

"*Neev*," Golden Man repeated. "That's an interesting name. Yet you sound like an American, yes?"

"It's Irish. I'm Irish-American. And my grandda owns—owned—this place." I gestured around me.

Both of golden man's eyebrows shot straight up. "Gallagher—of course. You're his granddaughter? I didn't know he had a granddaughter."

Golden Man sounded almost confounded, like he'd searched Grandda's Facebook already and hadn't found any random grandchildren in his friends list. (Okay, Grandda definitely hadn't been on Facebook. I'd checked years ago.)

"Why are you here?" Golden Man's gray eyes narrowed.

Now I was annoyed. What was it to him? Frowning, I said, "Yeah, I'm his granddaughter. And I'm here to see his lawyer. Not that it's any of your business."

"Ah," was all he said. He said it with a slight shrug, which felt so dismissive that my annoyance only grew.

I suddenly wished I hadn't said anything. I didn't need to explain myself to some random gardener. It didn't matter how pretty he was. The spell he'd cast on me broke, dousing me in figurative cold water.

"Okay, well, I'm going to go," I said, rather lamely.

I turned to leave, but Golden Man said, "Be careful, Miss Gallagher."

That was it. *Be careful.* I marveled at how confidently he said those words.

"That's it? You're not going to tell me why?" I crossed my arms under my breasts, my nose wrinkled. "How helpful of you."

Golden Man's gaze flicked to my cleavage as quickly as it returned to my face. He smiled when he noticed that I'd seen him, but it wasn't a friendly smile.

"You seem intelligent enough to understand what I meant," he said.

Before I could demand to know Golden Man's name and why he felt the need to be rude to his deceased employer's granddaughter, I heard the robot-butler say behind me, "Miss Gallagher? There you are. Mr. McDonnell has been looking for you for the past twenty minutes."

Golden Man had returned to his post, and I watched him for a moment longer as he pruned some fancy-looking bush full of red flowers.

Golden Man's identity would have to wait—for now.

CHAPTER TWO

It was still early morning, and I had hours to kill before I could meet with Mr. McDonnell later that afternoon. My stomach rumbled ominously. I hadn't eaten since I'd gotten on the plane over nine hours ago, and I was on the verge of getting full-on hangry.

But I had no idea how I went about feeding myself in this place. Did I just...go to the kitchen? Or would some red-cheeked cook tell me to get lost? *This isn't Downton Abbey,* I reminded myself. *And you're hardly Lady Mary who's never made a cup of coffee on her own.*

I got dressed and, after asking an unsuspecting maid where the kitchen was located, made my way downstairs. I was afraid I'd gotten lost when I smelled food. I headed toward the scent of cooking meat, my mouth practically watering.

Before you got to the main part of the kitchen, there was a smaller entranceway that looked like a gigantic pantry. There were cans and bags of all kinds of food, along with fresh produce in baskets. I snagged a banana and began to eat it.

As I moved farther into the kitchen, I could hear food sizzling and what sounded like a coffeepot dinging that coffee was ready. There was a large wood stove in one corner, although it clearly hadn't been used in decades. Windows lined the other side of the huge room, and I could just make out the white caps of the ocean waves.

I heard voices from around the corner to a smaller part of the kitchen that held what looked like the dishwasher and sink. A tall, skinny woman was saying something to a young man who couldn't have been much older than me. They didn't see me lurking until I cleared my throat.

The woman swiveled her head toward me. Honestly, she swiveled it so fast that I half-expected her to turn it 180 degrees like an owl. She narrowed her eyes at me.

"Who are you?" She looked at my sweats, my puppy slippers, and my oversized hoodie and said before I could answer, "You're the American."

"Um, hi. I was hungry, so I thought I'd get some breakfast." I held up my already half-eaten banana, as if I needed to prove that, yes, I was hungry and consuming food on the premises.

The woman's eyes narrowed at the banana in my hand. "I was going to use those for a fruit salad today," she said.

The young guy at her elbow coughed into his shoulder and sauntered past me, whispering, "Good luck," under his breath.

"Sorry. I didn't know." I held out the banana. "I don't need it—"

"I'm not going to cook with a banana you've already *eaten.*"

9

Now I felt especially stupid. What was I doing? Flustered, I was close to tossing the banana in the trash and running back to my room, but I forced myself to take a deep breath. I set the stupid banana on a nearby counter and held out my hand. "I'm Niamh Gallagher." Added in a harder tone, "Sean Gallagher's granddaughter."

The woman clucked her tongue. "I know who you are, lass." She didn't take my hand, though. She just kept staring at me, like she'd never seen someone like me in her life.

I was rather tempted to turn around and return to my room, but my stubbornness overtook my brain. It was one of my more admirable traits, in my opinion. Liam had learned early on that when I started to dig in my heels, he'd just have to give in.

(Okay, maybe he hadn't yet learned that, as he could be just as stubborn. Oftentimes we'd just end up trying to out-stubborn each other until somebody told us to stop being idiots.)

"I'm sorry, you didn't tell me your name," I said, knowing full well she hadn't introduced herself yet.

"Mrs. Janie Walsh." She wiped her hands on her towel before turning away from me to continuing kneading some kind of dough.

"Did you know my grandda?" I knew Mrs. Walsh was busy, but I couldn't help myself. The butler wasn't going to tell me anything, and neither was Mr. McDonnell, either.

Mrs. Walsh pounded at the bread dough. "I've worked at this place for almost four decades. Aye, you could say I knew him."

Forty years? That was dedication. "I didn't know him. I left Ireland when I was really little."

She looked up at me for a brief moment, her expression wry. "You're a chatty thing, aren't you?" She returned to her task, clearly very well-versed with kneading dough. "Your grandda was a hardheaded man, but he treated his staff well. That was enough for me."

"He wasn't all that fond of my brother, Liam."

"He wasn't fond of anyone." Mrs. Walsh let out a breath. "Well, except for his dear wife, your grandmother. What a dear lady she was. Never high in the instep, either. When she died, I don't think he ever recovered."

I'd never heard much about my grandmother. She'd died long before either Liam or I was born, and given our father's disappearance, I'd had no way to find out more about her. All I knew was that her name had been Mary and she'd died when she was in her early thirties.

"He loved her? That's kind of hard to believe."

Mrs. Walsh just gave me a withering look.

I shrugged. "He wasn't particularly kind to my brother or to our da." Trying to sound casual, I added, "Did you know my da? Connor Gallagher?"

At the mention of my da's name, Mrs. Walsh's face instantly closed, like a door slamming shut. She turned to open the oven, and after placing the bread inside, she closed the door with a surprisingly loud *thwack*.

Turning back to me, she said, "Lass, there are many things you don't know, and if you want some advice, let me give you some." Brushing the flour from her hands, she said before I could reply, "Don't ask too many questions. Some secrets are meant to stay that way."

She didn't give me a chance to respond. Feeling a frisson of ice slither down my spine, I rubbed at the goosebumps springing up on my arms.

Geez, what the hell had that advice meant? Now I was half-wondering if there was a dead body under the floorboards like that Edgar Allen Poe story. *Please, no dead bodies whispering to me. I really don't have time for that.*

But if Mrs. Walsh had known my da, then maybe she had information that could help me find him. I was about to follow her and badger her, but a young woman with red hair came around the corner, nearly hitting me in the chest with a cookie sheet with freshly baked buns.

"Oh, fuck!" The girl nearly lost her hold of the sheet in her hand. I grabbed the end closest to me, and luckily only one bun slid off of it onto the floor.

"Sorry, sorry." I reached down to pick up the bun. I brushed it off. "Five-second rule?"

The girl's face turned as red as her hair. "Oh, you're the American! Mr. Gallagher's granddaughter! I'm so sorry for cursing, miss—"

Good lord, I'd fallen into some kind of *Downton Abbey* RPG, hadn't I? If she called me "milady," I'd throw myself off of the nearest high cliff.

"Don't apologize. I was the one who nearly made you drop all of these buns." I peered more closely at the one in my hand. "What are these?"

"Bannock buns with currants, miss."

The one I was holding was still warm. Definitely better than just a banana. "Oh, excellent." I was about to take a bite, but the girl let out a squawk.

"Don't eat that! It fell on the floor." She set the sheet pan down, shaking her head, and went to get a plate. She plucked the contaminated bun from my hand and tossed it into the trash before giving me a fresh one on a plate. "Do you want butter with it, miss? And perhaps some tea or coffee?"

"Coffee, please. And please: call me Niamh. What's your name?"

The girl dimpled as she hurried to get me my order. "I'm Cara." She soon handed me a cup of steaming coffee and placed some pats of butter and a knife on my plate. "Lovely to meet you."

Cara had light freckles all over her nose, and a rosebud mouth with reddish eyebrows. She looked like she'd stepped out of a storybook, her skin creamy and fair.

"Is there anything I can get you?" she said.

"No, thank you." I collected my plate and coffee. "I'm glad somebody around here is nice," I said offhandedly.

"Oh?"

"I ran into Mrs. Walsh." I made sure to pitch my voice into a low whisper. "She's terrifying."

Cara's lips twitched. "Is she?"

"Um, yes? I think she would've loved to have put a curse on me, if she were into that sort of thing."

"I'm pretty certain she's a devoted Catholic." Cara's tone sounded strangled.

"She's got witchy vibes. I'm telling you. Probably rides here on a broomstick."

"I think she prefers to take the tram. Much more comfortable, especially when it rains."

I shrugged. "That's just what she tells people, I'm sure."

Cara giggled then covered her mouth. "I need to

return to my work. It was nice meeting you, miss—I mean, Niamh."

She hurried off. I'd probably gone too far with the joke about Mrs. Walsh being a witch. Maybe I'd offended Cara. *Great job, Niamh. Let's not alienate the one nice person you've met here.*

Thinking about not-nice people, I thought of the golden-haired man I'd met yesterday. That had been a strange encounter, to say the least. I just hoped I wouldn't keep running into him. He didn't have time for obnoxious men who thought way too highly of themselves.

You don't have time for men in general. Fair enough. My dating life was hardly interesting lately. What with attending Harvard and working my ass off to keep my grades up, graduating, and then moving back to Seattle, I'd been busy the past few years. I'd dated a few different guys while in college, the longest relationship lasting a year. Noah had been my first—first love, first time having sex. We'd met in a chemistry class and had been paired up as lab partners.

Noah had been sweet—too sweet. He'd been too easy to run roughshod over. It wasn't that I wanted to boss people around, but I had what my best friend Rachel said was a *commanding presence.* "Guys think you're intimidating," she'd said when I'd been frustrated with how wishy washy Noah had acted. "He probably doesn't know what to do with you."

She'd been right. I'd eventually broken things off with Noah because he'd gotten, well, boring. When I'd wanted to have long conversations into the night, he'd wanted to play video games for hours instead. When I'd known I'd always wanted to major in political science, he'd switched majors every semester. And when he'd teared up when I broke up with him, I felt like I'd literally kicked a puppy.

I'd had two other shorter relationships that had amounted mostly to a friends-with-benefits type of situation. But none of them had held my attention. The sex had been decent and was nice to scratch that itch. Yet after a few sex sessions, I'd feel kind of...empty. Not that I'd regretted sleeping with them, just that I wanted more than something surface-level.

So, I hadn't dated much in the past year. I was only twenty-two, of course, but sometimes I felt like I'd never find a guy who was worth my time. And I struggled not to dumb myself down, to make myself less intimidating, whatever that actually meant.

The rest of the day, I wandered the estate. I got lost more than once, and I had to ask staff to point me in the right direction. Multiple times I'd tried to open doors that were locked, so I contented myself with looking at all of the artwork and sculptures throughout the house.

I didn't run into Golden Man again. By the end of the day, I almost wished I had. I'd only had interactions with people who treated me like their mistress, and it had made me feel weird.

I finally just returned to my room and read until it was late enough to go to bed, all the while telling myself I hadn't made a mistake in coming here.

CHAPTER THREE

I shifted in bed, trying to find a comfortable position, but despite the silky sheets and a mattress that could've easily fit four adults, I couldn't fall asleep. Sighing, I sat up in bed and rubbed my temples.

"Stupid jet lag," I muttered to myself. I'd even taken a Benadryl, but all it had done was make me feel fuzzy-headed. Gulping down a glass of water, I went to sit in front of the fireplace—no fire, it was the middle of summer, after all—and after turning on a light tried to read a book.

But my brain kept bouncing from subject to subject. After I'd encountered Golden Man, I'd met with Mr. McDonnell.

Months ago, Mr. McDonnell had written me a letter to inform me that Grandda had left me more than just the inheritance that had paid for my college education. When I'd written back via email, because this was the twenty-first century after all, Mr. McDonnell had sent his reply once again on actual paper.

I didn't understand his drive to waste money on

postage, but perhaps he had more trust for the postal systems of Ireland and the United States than he did his internet provider.

At any rate, he'd told me that if I were to receive this inheritance, I'd have to come to Ireland myself to claim it. *It had been your grandfather's wish for you to do so,* Mr. McDonnell had written in curling script.

Oh, had I mentioned he'd handwritten those letters? I was half-convinced he'd walked straight out of an Austen novel.

Apparently, according to Mr. McDonnell, my grandda had been an odd sort, and this had been his last demand before he'd died. Considering that he'd died four years ago, it had seemed odd to me that I'd only gotten this missive earlier this year.

I closed the book I was failing to read. Even the smuttiest of smut couldn't hold my attention tonight. Getting up, I went to the window of my expansive bedroom. The window overlooked the stairs and, just on the horizon, the black waters of the Irish Sea. The moon was silvery white, full and shining on the waters like a beacon.

The meeting with Mr. McDonnell had been short. He'd only needed to inform me that my additional inheritance was, in fact, the entire estate. Yes, really.

"Are you serious?" I'd stared at the lawyer in confusion, hardly believing his last words.

"Yes, miss." Mr. McDonnell had cleared his throat. "But there's a complication, you see."

"Oh, lovely."

He'd ignored my sarcasm. "You see, your grandfather was…an interesting sort of man." He pulled out an envelope, much like the one I'd received from Mr.

McDonnell all those months ago. "Well, he can explain himself better than I can."

Frowning, I ripped open the envelope, unfolding the thick parchment.

To my granddaughter,

By now, you must've met with Mr. McDonnell in person. He most likely has now given you this letter because he's incapable of explaining things himself. He's a useful sort but not clever.

Let's not waste time. I hardly have any left, to be sure.

Your father is alive, and before you ask, I've always known he was alive. I didn't inform you of this fact because, quite frankly, I doubted that it mattered. A more useless, moronic individual than your father I've never known. He threw away everything to marry your mother and then decided he'd had enough and abandoned his entire family. Why, you may ask? I don't know, nor do I particularly care, either.

This letter is to tell you that, as my only heir that is worth a bloody damn (your fool brother squandered the opportunity to inherit years ago, as you're well aware), you can inherit this estate and everything inside of it if you find your father and give him a letter Mr. McDonnell will provide to you after you read this one.

I'm sure you're wondering: where is my godforsaken son? I don't know. I wasn't able to discover his location before my illness made me unable to do anything but pray to God that I wouldn't spend all eternity in Purgatory. Now it's up to you, Granddaughter. If you're at all clever and capable, you can find your father. If you cannot find him, then suffice to say this estate will go up for auction and most likely bought by some English arsehole looking for a summer home for his sallow-faced children.

Yours,

Sean Gallagher

If the ground had dropped out from under me

before, I was now hurtling into a black hole into space. Hope, along with dismay, made it impossible to speak.

Da was alive. He was alive, and Grandda had known.

I wish I could strangle you myself, I thought bitterly. *No wonder Liam hated your guts. You wily old asshole. Even from beyond the grave, you're trying to mess with us.*

I stared dumbly down at the paper in my hand for such a long time that Mr. McDonnell finally cleared his throat to get my attention.

"Are you quite well, Miss Gallagher?"

"My da is alive?" was all that I could say.

"Indeed. You haven't been in contact with him in a number of years. Is that correct?"

I shook my head. "He left us before I was even born."

Mr. McDonnell shuffled some papers, looking extremely uncomfortable.

I barely registered his discomfort. My heart was clamoring in my chest. I wanted to ask every question under the sun, all the while knowing that it was unlikely this lawyer would have the answers. I doubted Mr. McDonnell could tell me why my da had abandoned his family and had never tried to contact us again.

While Liam had been content to believe our da was six feet under, I'd never stopped wondering about him. We only had a handful of photos of him; Liam had torn up a bunch of them when he'd been an angry teenager, never thinking that his little sister might have an interest in our deadbeat father.

Since Mam had died when I'd been so young, I'd always longed to know about Da. The thought that I still had one parent alive was strangely comforting. And, in that hope that only a child could have, maybe he'd have a reason as to why he'd had to stay away from us.

Now as an adult, I knew very well that it was pretty unlikely that he'd gone into hiding because he was a spy or because the mafia was out to kill him. I couldn't blame some shadowy villain for my da being a deadbeat, yet that still didn't stop the need to ask him in person the question: *why did you leave and never come back?*

"So how exactly am I supposed to find my da?"

"I have some information that we were able to gather regarding his whereabouts." Mr. McDonnell handed me another envelope, painfully slim. "Your father has not wanted to be found. I will say that."

"That doesn't answer my question." Frustration tinged my voice. I'd already Googled my da multiple times, but his name was a common one in Ireland. Even if I'd found records of him, it didn't mean I could discover his latest address without a lot of digging.

"We received this about two years ago. As you can see, it was addressed to your grandfather, but of course, he was no longer with us to open it."

In the corner of the manila envelope was the name of some appraisal company here in Ireland. Confused, I opened the envelope to find a few documents that contained something about an antique clock that had been appraised two years ago by Sean Gallagher, my dead grandda.

The clock was made of porcelain and covered in ormolu. At the top was a painting of a cherub with a laurel wreath adorning the miniature; below was another cherub, an acorn adorning it at the bottom. A sky was painted in the center of the clock face.

Most tellingly, the appraisal price of this clock was

listed at a staggering €25,000. My eyes nearly bugged out of my head seeing that.

"Okay, somebody has a freaking expensive clock somewhere. What does this have to do with my da?"

"The signature on the last page," said Mr. McDonnell, not the least bit fazed by my confusion. He pushed another document toward me across the desk. "It matches your father's."

"But the name listed is for Sean, not Connor," I countered.

"Your father's full name is Sean Connor Gallagher. And if you notice the first name of the signature on that document…"

I peered more closely at the scribble. It looked like someone had begun to write a *C* but had awkwardly changed it to an *S*, as if remembering what his name really was.

"I realize this is extremely strange and not absolute proof that your father is alive, but considering your grandfather had had located him five years ago in Spain, it doesn't seem impossible he'd still be alive just three years later."

I placed the appraisal documents back inside the envelope. Okay, so my da was most likely alive. "But no one knows where he is now? Or within the last year?"

"I'm afraid not, miss."

Of course not. That'd be too easy. "Why would these documents be sent here and not to my da's address?"

Mr. McDonnell shrugged. "I'm not certain why he'd forge his signature, but from the bit of research I was able to do, the clock itself is an antique once owned by Mr. Connor Gallagher's mother. Perhaps he wanted to send a message to Mr. Sean Gallagher that he'd acquired it."

"But my grandda was dead by then."

"Yes, but perhaps your father did not know that."

It seemed as plausible a theory as any. None of the men in my family had been fond of my grandda, it seemed. Sean Gallagher had hated that his only son and heir had married beneath him, and then he'd apparently hated his son even more for leaving the wife he'd never approved of.

Talk about complicated family history. It made my head hurt to think about it.

"Although I have not been able to locate your father," said Mr. McDonnell, "logic seems to point in the direction that if you can locate this antique clock, you most likely can locate Mr. Connor."

I let out a sigh. "I never knew my da, but given how my brother always talked about him, I have a feeling he'd enjoy making us go on a wild goose chase to find him." Holding my grandda's letter and the appraisal documents, I asked, "May I keep these?"

"Of course, miss."

Now, staring at the fireplace sans fire, I shook my head. I'd nearly choked on my own spit when Mr. McDonnell had told me that. Me, the owner of all of *this?* It made zero sense.

Grandda hadn't known me. He'd disliked Liam simply because Liam had never been a good, submissive Catholic who'd cater to Grandda's every demand. When Liam had taken me from Ireland when I was six and he

22

was twenty-three, apparently Grandda had been livid. When he'd told us about our inheritances when we came of age, he'd punished Liam by giving him a piddly amount while giving me ten times that when I'd turned eighteen.

It was strange, being beholden to a man I'd not really known and who was now, even from the grave, pulling the strings in my own family. I was sure wherever he was, he was enjoying making us squirm.

As far as our father, Connor Gallagher, he'd been disinherited and disowned after he'd married our mother without Grandda's permission. So even if he was still alive, he wouldn't have gotten a penny from Grandda anyway. *He really loved disinheriting people,* I thought wryly.

Looking at my phone, I considered calling my brother for advice. It was only six in the evening in Seattle. But Liam would be worried if I called him in the middle of the night, and he and his wife Mari would be busy with getting the girls dinner and then to bed. I didn't want to add to their stress.

I sighed. I wrapped myself in a robe and put on some slippers, wondering if a late-night stroll would calm my mind. Although part of me felt weird about wandering around a house that wasn't mine, I reasoned that it was *almost* mine. Besides, everyone was asleep, and I was just going to wander the hallways.

Dim lights turned on as I walked. I stopped a few times to admire artwork hanging on the walls. Some were more traditional paintings of what I guessed were Irish landscapes. Others were more *avant garde*, splotches of color that weren't depicting anything except maybe chaos. Looking at one that could've been painted by my four-year-old niece Fiona, I had a distinct feeling that Grandda wasn't the one buying these pieces. He would've hated this one.

I wandered for a while longer, coming to a hallway I hadn't been down. As I walked, I saw that a door was open, and I peered inside to see a library. The moon was the only light, although more lights turned as I began to wander the aisles.

Had my grandda been a big reader? I wondered. One aisle had books that were all written in Irish. I pulled one out, curious, but my Irish was rudimentary at best, and I could hardly read a heavy tome that seemed to be about Ireland's flora and fauna.

Other aisles had books in English, most of which seemed to be nonfiction: natural history of Ireland, Catholic treatises, and a variety of Bibles were all collected together. I did finally find a section of fiction, most of the authors being Irish—James Joyce, Samuel Beckett, Oscar Wilde were all there.

I pulled out a collection of Yeats' poems. I flipped it open to find an inscription at the front in Irish that I was able to translate: *to my beloved Maire, Sean.* I knew that Maire was the Irish version of Mary.

My heart started pounding. It felt like kismet, coming upon this book dedicated to my grandmother after that strange conversation I'd had with Mrs. Walsh.

I flipped through the pages, and my heart nearly fell to my toes when a note fluttered to the floor. I grabbed it, noting that edges were yellow with age. I carefully unfolded it after I'd set the book down on a nearby table.

I squinted at the handwriting. It was in Irish, I realized, so I could only make out a few words that I remembered learning as a child. Liam could still speak Irish; he'd lived here in Ireland until he was twenty-three. Whereas I'd left when I was only six and he'd placed me in the care of my uncle Henry and aunt Siobhan, Siobhan being our mother's younger sister. Siobhan had never learned Irish, and I'll admit, I hadn't had much discipline to take classes when I was younger.

Now I desperately wished I'd learned the language. The letter was from my grandmother Mary to Sean, dated over seventy years ago.

I carefully folded the letter up again and placed it back inside the book. I would take a photo of it and send it to Liam to see if he could read it and translate it for me. I had no idea how good his reading skills in Irish were these days. For all I knew, he could only speak it and understand it orally.

I could always try to translate it myself, I reasoned. I mean, did I really want Liam involved? He might not be all that gung-ho about a letter written to our grandda, unless the contents were basically the Irish version of "go fuck yourself."

Well, Google Translate could at least give me the gist of it, I told myself.

Snagging the book, I was about to go back to my room when I heard a noise to my left. I hadn't realized that there was a smaller wooden door, partially open, that led to another part of the library.

I heard another noise, and my heart started pounding. I considered just scurrying back to my room, but a part of me felt stupid for being afraid. It could just be a rat or this old house creaking from the wind. *It's probably ghosts*, my mind whispered, only half-joking.

I opened the small door. There were no lights on in

the room, although I couldn't tell if the lights installed were motion-detected like the ones in the hallways. I listened intently, still clutching the books of Yeats' poems, when I heard a thump.

I froze. It was the middle of the night. Would any of the workers even be here at this hour? Despite its *Downton Abbey* feel, the estate didn't actually house the people who worked here, at least according to the butler Roger, whose name I'd finally learned today. He'd told me that everyone returned home by the end of the day like any other employee going home from the office. The exception being the lone security guard that sat in a tiny office at the front gate, waving people in without so much as looking up from his iPad.

I waited, listening intently. And then I heard the squeak of door hinges, and then it was complete silence.

Who knew how long I stood there in the dark, clutching my book, my heart hammering in my throat? When I finally told myself that whoever had been in here was gone, I practically ran back to my room and bolted the door behind me.

Maybe Roger hadn't meant that every single person went home? There could still be *someone* working here. Maybe it had been the security guard. But why would he be in the library? That made no sense.

Shivering, I got in bed, pulled the covers up to my chin, and failed miserably to fall asleep.

CHAPTER FOUR

The next morning, I considered calling Liam to tell him about the stranger in the library but then thought better of it. My older brother was *way* overprotective. Knowing him, he'd fly straight here to pummel somebody—anybody.

Instead, I called Rachel, who'd been my roommate my last two years at Harvard and who now lived in New York City with her girlfriend Maddie. She was one of the most levelheaded people I knew. I could tell her that I'd met five blue aliens and we'd all gotten high on bath salts and eaten our weight in fish and chips, and she wouldn't bat an eyelash.

First of all, I gave her the short version of what I'd learned from Mr. McDonnell about my father and the mysterious clock I was now supposed to search for.

"Do you even know what the clock looks like?" said Rachel.

I was currently sitting outside, my cup of coffee having already gone cold from the chill wind blowing off of the water. "Um, I have no idea. It's a clock. I'm assuming it has two hands and numbers on it."

Rachel snorted. "Well, duh. But what's it made of? What century is it from? Is it super fancy and gold-plated, or wooden, or…?"

"I really doubt it matters."

"Well, the more information you have on this clock, the more information you could possibly get to find your da."

I chewed on my bottom lip. "That sounds very logical and smart, and I'm annoyed that I didn't think of it first."

"That's why you're friends with me." I could hear the smugness in her voice, the jerk.

"But why would my da, who's pretty much hidden himself away from his family for twenty-plus years now, suddenly want his da to know he still exists? Although I guess he failed, considering that my grandda was already dead by the time those papers were mailed."

I could hear Rachel moving around in her apartment. "Tuna, stop!" she yelled in the background. "Will you stop chewing on the stupid blinds?" She sighed into the phone. "This cat, I swear."

"I think he's just mad you named him something he loves to eat."

"He doesn't even like tuna! But he's obsessed with eating popcorn. It makes no sense."

I not so subtly forced Rachel back to the subject at hand. "What's your theory on my da's motives?"

"Either he knew your grandfather was already dead and wanted to keep his identity secret or he wanted your grandfather to know he'd gotten that clock," she said.

I frowned. "It doesn't make much sense that my da

wanted to conceal his identity by using an identity that's directly linked to him."

"Hey, I never said it was a *good* idea."

We discussed the strange circumstances a while longer, but neither of us really had any idea where I was going to start looking for my da, beyond finding out more information about this clock. There hadn't been much identifying information about the antique in the paperwork Mr. McDonnell had given me, but admittedly, I'd only skimmed it. Perhaps there was some nugget of information—a brand name? serial number? —that could provide a clue.

After we'd exhausted the clock conversation, I recounted my strange encounter in the library the night before.

"Are you sure you heard someone walking around? Maybe it was just the house making noises," said Rachel.

"I'm pretty sure creaky old house noises are way different than footsteps." Irritation crept into my voice. "Besides, I heard a door close."

She made a humming noise. "Fair enough. I mean, it could've been an intruder, but at the same time, lots of people work there."

"You don't think it's weird?"

"Kinda, but not really?"

"It was almost three AM!"

"True, but you were there, too. So someone else had the same idea as you. It sounds like a weird coincidence, that's all."

I sighed. "But wouldn't they have said something? Why act shady if you aren't, in fact, doing something shady?"

I could practically hear Rachel shrugging. An econ major, Rachel preferred to live her life according to logic and numbers. Sometimes it felt like she didn't care, but I'd known her long enough now that she *did* care. She just showed it differently. When she worked through the logic of your situation, it meant she wanted to find the answer to help you.

But sometimes I wished she'd be more emotional. Sometimes you just needed somebody to tell you that your feelings were valid, you know? Then again, it wasn't like Rachel was my therapist. I couldn't exactly expect her to act like one.

"Well, I think this means you need to go back there tonight to see if the person returns," Rachel said finally.

"I don't really want to wait up all night." I snorted at the image. "Sitting in some huge armchair, rifle in hand, waiting for some unsuspecting random to wander in—"

"Hey, I didn't say anything about a gun."

"And turns it out it was just poor Roger, caught sleepwalking again."

Rachel chuckled. "Don't shoot the butler. Pretty sure you'll get seven years of bad luck for that one."

We chatted for a bit longer, Rachel telling me about the classes she planned to take when she began her grad program in the fall at NYU. Her girlfriend Maddie was in her second year of medical school at Columbia. Yes, both of these women were ridiculously impressive, and, yes, I often felt like a big weird loser compared to them both.

"Oh, Maddie, say hi to Niamh," said Rachel.

"Hi, Niamh," I heard Maddie call from the background. "Don't forget to bring back some Guinness for me!"

"I won't forget," I said with a laugh before we said our goodbyes.

I realized only after I'd hung up that I hadn't told her about the obnoxious golden-haired man I'd met. It'd only been a few days, yet it felt like that had happened an eternity ago.

What if the library intruder was Golden Man? my brain asked me. But he was a gardener. There was no reason he'd be lurking around the estate late at night.

Well, unless he was looking for something. Or he just really wanted to borrow some books and didn't feel like asking for permission. But why do it in the middle of the night?

"It probably was a ghost," I muttered to myself as I made my way back inside, the cold making me shiver. "Or you just imagined it."

Even as I said the words aloud, I knew I didn't believe them. I also knew that the library was probably the best way for me to find more information about this stupid clock, so I'd need to return there tonight. Although not at three AM. I'd go there at a reasonable hour, so at the very least, if someone jumped out of the shadows to attack me, there were still employees around to (hopefully) hear me scream.

On my way back to my room, I ran into Cara. "Oh, I can take that," she said, taking my cold mug of coffee. "Do you want another cup? Or I could warm this one up for you."

I had to restrain myself from cringing. It felt way too weird to have this girl, who was probably around my age, treat me like I was her mistress. Even though I guess for all intents and purposes, I would be inheriting the money to pay these people's salaries. That alone made me feel like I'd been doused in cold water.

"No, I'm okay, thanks." As Cara was about to continue on her way, I said, "Wait. I have a question."

"Yes?"

"Who all works here at night?"

She raised a ginger eyebrow. "At night? It's mostly a skeleton staff until after dinner is served. Most everyone goes home around nine PM, except for the security guard."

"So there's no one here at, say, three in the morning?"

Cara gave me a strange look. "Not that I know of. Why do you ask?"

I didn't know why I didn't tell her about my library encounter right then and there, but something made me keep my mouth shut. Maybe I just didn't want to deal with a bunch of people questioning me.

Or maybe I wanted to confront this person myself, instead of he or she scampering off when they caught wind of an investigation.

Yeah, that'll end well, Niamh. You're totally Sherlock Holmes and know exactly what you're doing.

"I was just curious," I said, trying to sound casual. "I was hungry in the middle of the night, but I didn't want to scare anyone going down to the kitchen."

If Cara wasn't convinced, she was too polite to say it out loud. "May I give you some advice?" she said instead.

"Of course."

Her eyes sparkled now. "If you go into the kitchen at night, don't leave anything for Mrs. Walsh to find in the morning. She's a tad territorial."

"Now I'm imagining her transforming into the Hulk if she finds a dirty plate on the counter."

"You're not far off."

For the rest of the day, I spent it in the library. I brought the letters and documents Mr. McDonnell had already given me, going over them with a fine-tooth comb. I also brought the book of poetry I'd found inscribed to my grandmother and the note enclosed inside.

The documents about the purchase of the clock listed the clock, signed by Jean-Louis Lambert. After some Googling, I discovered that the clockmaker had been a fairly illustrious one in late eighteenth-century France. Lambert had made clocks for a number of aristocrats, and one had even been commissioned by King Louis XVI for Queen Marie Antoinette.

But when the Terror swept through the country, Lambert was, unfortunately, decried as a traitor, and he barely escaped with his life. As far as anyone knew, he'd spent the last few years of his life in England before dying penniless.

So this clock was French and definitely had a lot of history attached to it. But why would my da want it? No one in my family was French, as far as I knew. On my father's side, everyone was Irish, at least as far as I knew.

I opened the page in the poetry book to the inscription to my grandmother. Considering I knew nothing about her, my grandmother Mary could've been French. She could've been Russian, or from the moon, for all I knew about her.

I touched the lines of ink. It was strange to think of

my grandda, always a terrifying figure in my imagination, as a man who'd been in love with his wife.

Sean Gallagher had been a controlling force in my life and Liam's even though I'd never met the man. When Liam had married his wife, Mari, on a drunken night in Las Vegas, Liam had tried to make everyone think the marriage was real so as not to invoke the wrath of our grandda. Because if Grandda had found out, he would've taken away my inheritance out of a fit of pique—or so Liam thought.

Please know that I knew nothing about this, and when Liam finally spilled his guts to me, I told him he was a complete idiot. Fortunately for me, I still got the money, and now I was getting this estate. So I guess Liam had been right—not that I'd ever tell my brother that.

I began to look for any more information about Lambert, but despite looking through what felt like hundreds of books, there wasn't any reference to him or to this clock that I could find in my grandda's collection.

I changed course. I input the letter written in Irish into Google Translate. It was slow work, as the handwriting was difficult to decipher and a number of the letters had accents above them. I decided to do the translation one sentence at a time, in case I hadn't transcribed a word accurately and needed to correct it.

When the entire letter had been translated, my heart was almost pounding out of my chest with excitement. The letter itself wasn't particularly interesting, except for the last line that included the word *clock*.

My grandmother had owned a clock that apparently my grandda had given her. There was nothing else about it contained in the letter, but it had to be the clock that my da now had. I mean, what were the odds that there were two different ones?

I must've been a family heirloom of some sort. "Grandma, who were you?" I whispered under my breath as I scribbled notes. "Because I'm pretty sure you're the key to everything."

But when my stomach growled, I realized that the sun had already set and I hadn't eaten in almost ten hours. I glanced at my phone: it was a quarter till nine o'clock. I could either wait for the staff to leave for the day or venture downstairs and hope Mrs. Walsh would be nice enough to give me some spare crumbs for dinner.

I collected the notes, papers, and books, not wanting to risk leaving them for someone to rifle through. Especially if the random stranger returned tonight to the library.

I must've not been paying enough attention, though, because it was right before I was about to go to sleep that I realized I must've left the book of poetry in the library. It was just before midnight.

"Hopefully I won't have another run-in," I murmured to myself as I made my way back to the library. I'll admit, every creaking sound I heard made me nearly jump out of my skin. I nearly picked up a vase to throw at a dark corner, only to realize the sound I was hearing was the wind whistling outside.

CHAPTER FIVE

The library was large enough that it had more than one entrance. The entrance where I'd worked that afternoon was closer to my bedroom. Opening the door slowly, I peeked my head inside, but it was dark. I strained for any sounds, but once again, all I could hear was the wind.

I blew out a breath. I needed to calm down, clearly. I flipped on a lamp on a nearby desk and went to grab the book. It had somehow fallen under the table I'd been working at. I crouched down to retrieve it when I heard a sound.

This time, it wasn't the wind. It was a door opening, but not the one I'd just gone through. As I listened, I heard footsteps and the faint creaking of boards.

My heart was hammering. I realized I'd left the desk lamp light on, but if I turned it off now, it would alert the intruder to my presence.

And because I was an idiot, apparently, I was too slow to slip out the door, because the footsteps were getting closer to my hiding place. I was now hiding behind an armchair as I watched the shadowy figure make their way to a chest of drawers on the opposite wall. The person's back was turned, but I was pretty sure it was a man. And that man was now trying to open one of the drawers, muttering under his breath when it proved to be locked.

So much for my theory that he was probably harmless or a servant looking for a book to read. Anger spiked within me. How dare he try to steal from my grandda? From *me?*

I was torn between calling the police and just staying hidden until the man left when he began moving closer to where I was hiding. I had no escape route now. Panicking, I jumped from my hiding place, raised the book I'd retrieved, and hit the intruder upside the head.

"*Merde!*" The figure staggered backward, clutching at their head. Something thumped onto the floor.

I was sweating and panting, wishing I'd been smart enough to return to my room. I turned to run, but it was dark enough in the room that I didn't see the person's foot right next to me. I went tumbling, landing on top of them. Based on the low voice, they were most likely male.

"Let me go!" I was saying, pushing at his hands. "I'll scream—!"

He somehow maneuvered both of us so that I was underneath him. He clapped a hand over my mouth before I could scream. "I'm not going to hurt you," he said, his voice surprisingly calm. "Let me turn on a light."

I knew that voice: the Golden Man. I was still as he

rose, and then I was blinking like an owl when he turned on a light. He stood over me, a rueful smile on his handsome face. I could see the edge of a large bruise forming at his hairline from where I'd hit him.

"You!" I got up before he could offer me his hand.

He curled his fingers into his hand, an amused smile on his face. "You say that so accusingly." He rubbed at the spot on his head where I'd hit him. "What the hell did you hit me with? And why did you have to hit me so *hard?*"

"What do you think I hit you with in a library? A book."

"It felt more like a brick."

"I don't generally carry bricks around to hit people with as I'm exploring my grandda's house in the middle of the night."

"Now that's genuinely shocking."

I snorted, but as Golden Man rubbed at the bruise on his head, I felt guilty, too. I hoped I hadn't given him a concussion. It would just be my luck that I'd injure one of the staff before I'd even been here for twenty-four hours.

I swallowed my pride. "I'm sorry I hit you. Is it bad?"

"Hard to say. I should probably go to hospital all the same. I'm feeling rather dizzy, if I'm honest. Should I be seeing spots in my vision? Oh dear." He lurched forward toward a nearby chair.

I froze. "The hospital? Are you sure? Shit, I'm so, so sorry. Let me help you sit down——"

Golden Man started laughing, and his pained look disappeared in an instant. "You should see the expression on your face," he said, still laughing, hard enough that he was wiping tears from his eyes.

I stiffened my spine. "You—are you fucking serious right now?"

"About what, precisely?"

I growled. Grabbing the book of poetry, I lifted it threateningly. "I swear to God, do you need to go to the hospital or not? If you lie to me, I'll hit you again."

"What a vicious girl you are."

"Tell me!"

I was so focused on his answer that I didn't feel him pluck the book from my fingers before it was too late. "Yeats? Very appropriately Irish of you." He flipped through the pages, as if he had all the time in the world to choose a poem. He then began to read:

A mermaid found a swimming lad,
Picked him for her own,
Pressed her body to his body,
Laughed: and plunging down
Forgot in cruel happiness
That even lovers drown.

His accent made the words especially erotic, and it was like I could feel them against my skin. When he'd finished, his gaze was heated.

"Pretty mermaid, are you here to drown me?" he asked.

I felt like the world had tipped on its side. One minute I was afraid that I'd seriously injured this strange man; the next, he was practically propositioning me with poetry. Whatever happened to a "u up?" booty call message on Tinder? This guy was playing on an entirely new level compared to the men I'd dated.

"I'm not a mermaid." I tried to take the book back, but Golden Man's grip was stronger than I'd anticipated. "Give that back."

"If you say please." He smiled, his teeth white and straight and obnoxious.

I scowled. "How about I promise not to hit you again and give you an actual concussion instead?"

"Americans have a strange way of saying please."

Backed into a proverbial corner, I finally muttered *please*, very tempted to carry out my threat of hitting him a second time. Holding the book to my chest, I narrowed my eyes at the Golden Man.

"Why are you skulking about my grandda's library in the middle of the night?" I asked. In all the commotion, I'd yet to find out what the hell he was even doing here.

"I'd ask you the same question."

I rolled my eyes. "I'm the granddaughter of the owner." *And will soon own it out right*, I thought. "I don't have to tell you anything. You, however, work here, and based on our initial encounter, you have no reason to be in the library."

"Are you saying landscapers shouldn't have access to knowledge?" He clucked his tongue. "That's not very American of you. Aren't you all about equality and freedom—"

"Please shut up. You talk too much."

He just bowed.

"Now, stop trying to weasel your way out of answering my question. Why were you trying to go through those drawers? What are you trying to steal?" I held up my phone like it was a weapon. "I'll call the cops if you don't tell me. I doubt you want to go to jail tonight."

Golden Man just crossed his arms. He looked way too relaxed, although in the dim light, I could make out how tight his jaw was clenched. He held out his hands, even going so far as to pull out his pockets. "I've stolen nothing. What would be the charges?"

"Um, trespassing?"

"I work here."

"Not in the middle of the night. No one but the security guard does. I already confirmed that fact."

He chuckled. "Aren't you thorough?"

I didn't know the number for emergencies here in Ireland, but I began to dial 911 anyway. Hopefully my smartphone was actually smart enough to know what I meant.

As I tapped the 1 on my phone, Golden Man said, "Fine, fine! I'll tell you everything." He scowled. "Damn harpy woman," he muttered.

I decided I'd ignore that comment. Returning my phone to my robe's pocket, I gestured at the armchair I'd been hiding behind just minutes earlier. "Sit."

We sat down across from each other. Golden Man crossed his legs, waiting for me to begin the interrogation.

"How about we start with an easy question: what's your name? And *please*, don't give me some random answer that doesn't actually answer the question."

"My name is Olivier."

I waited for more, but Olivier didn't seem inclined to give me a last name. Fine. It was better than nothing.

"I'm Niamh," I said.

Olivier's lips twitched. "You already told me that. Or do you not remember our first meeting?"

"I've been so busy that it completely slipped my mind." My tone was sugar-sweet. "But now that I at least have a name for you, how about you tell me why you've been skulking around my grandda's library two nights in a row?"

"*Skulk*? I've never skulked in my life." He almost sounded genuinely offended.

"*Sneak*, then?" I pulled up the thesaurus on my phone just to be extra petty. "Oh, here we go: how about *snoop*? Wait, *creep* is a good one. You've definitely been creeping. A creep who's been sneakily skulking in *my* library—"

Olivier said something in what I presumed to be French, ruffling his hair as he sifted his fingers through it. "You're like a dog with a bone."

"If I need to, I'll sit on you until you tell me the truth. I have all night, mister."

I realized I'd made a technical error when his eyes flashed. "You make it sound like you sitting on my lap would be a burden. Not when I was done with you."

I was glad it was dark enough that he couldn't see me blushing like a teenage girl. "Stop flirting with me to distract me!" I was close to throwing the book still clutched in my hands at his big, dumb face. "Get on with your explanation!"

"You're not giving me much of a reason to be honest with you."

I just waited. He could either spill his guts, or I'd... do something. Hit him again with another, much heavier book. Maybe push him out a window. They'd never find his body once he hit the dark water below.

"I'm looking for something," said Olivier. "Something your grandfather had in his possession."

I propped my chin on my hand. "I figured that out much for myself," I said wryly.

Olivier rubbed at his head where I'd hit him with the book. He said something in French again—probably something about how women were evil she-demons. I'd admit, seeing him wince was immensely satisfying.

"I'm looking for an antique that your grandfather bought years ago. It's extremely important to my family."

My ears perked up. "An antique what?"

Olivier sat up slightly to pull out a folded piece of paper. He handed it to me, not needing to say the words "antique clock" because I'd already unfolded the paper to see the clock in question. The same exact clock that my *father*, not my grandfather, possessed.

My mind moved rapidly. Suddenly, things were becoming even more complicated than they had been just an hour ago. Why was this clock so valuable? Was it full of diamonds or something? Maybe it contained the key to some safe that was filled with gemstones. Or cocaine. Knowing my luck, it was probably full of cocaine.

"Okay," I said slowly. I handed him back the paper. "Why do you think my grandda has—had—this clock?"

"I can't divulge that information."

He said it so haughtily that I was tempted to hit him with my book a second time, but I refrained. I needed him conscious at this moment in time. Mostly, though, I had a feeling this Golden Man who'd randomly showed up in my grandda's library and who was looking for the exact same thing I was searching for was such an insane coincidence that I knew it couldn't be entirely a coincidence.

There was something about this clock that was more important than it being a family heirloom. What, exactly, I couldn't begin to guess.

"Well, my grandda is dead." I waved a hand. "And I haven't seen that clock anywhere in this house." Olivier didn't know that this was my first visit—probably. Hopefully.

"Yes, I realized that when I first arrived." Olivier steepled his fingers, his fingers long, his nails perfectly filed. Strange, for someone who supposedly worked with plants and dirt all day.

I knew in that moment I had two choices: I could keep the small nugget of information that I had about the clock in question—that my father was the one who had it—to myself. Or I could use it as a way to get Olivier to share *his* information.

I could hear my brother Liam's voice in my head. *Don't show your cards too soon. Let the other person wait. Sometimes patience is all that stands between you and victory, even if the chips are down.*

"I'm going to go out on a limb and say that you're not, in fact, a gardener."

Olivier looked at this steepled hands and grinned. "Guilty as charged. I got a job here on false pretenses, I admit it. I wanted to find out any information I could. Unfortunately, the one person who could've given me any information is dead." He shot me a look. "My condolences, of course."

"I didn't know him. Apparently, everybody who knew him hated him. My brother practically threw a party when we found out he'd died."

Olivier choked back a laugh, coughing into his fist to cover it. "Then I retract my condolences." His gaze went distant as he added, "This clock, though. It's extremely important to my family, to my mother especially. I promised her that I would find it for her." Something shadowy crossed over his face when he said those words, which, annoyingly enough, made him seem less of a fallen angel and more of an actual human being.

"It's funny that you're searching for this clock," I said slowly, "because I'm also looking for it. Although for a different reason."

Olivier's gaze landed on me, hard. "You know about it? How?"

"I'm not at leisure to disclose my sources," I said sweetly.

He looked at me for a longer moment, as if trying to understand my motives. I wasn't entirely certain of my own motives, beyond knowing that if this man was the key to finding my father, I'd use this opportunity, regardless of the consequences.

"I have a feeling you know what this all means," I said.

Olivier leaned back in his chair. "Do I?"

"Do I really need to say something straight out of *The Godfather*? 'I have a proposition you can't refuse.'"

"As long as I don't have a horse head in my bed in the morning, then I'll hear this proposition." His lips quirked. "I always enjoy women propositioning me."

I wanted to dunk his face in the nearest flower arrangement. "Keep your pants on, dude. I know who owns this clock you want, and if you agree to help me— help *us*—find it, I won't call the police and press charges for trespassing."

"You don't know if I have any more useful information," he pointed out.

"Then we'll go our separate ways and never think about the other person again."

Olivier considered me, stroking his bottom lip as he did so. It was strangely sensual, making heat curl in my belly. I barely restrained myself from squirming in my seat.

Look, I wasn't some naive virgin. I'd had sex. Okay, I could count on my hand how many times I'd had sex, but it *had* happened. So I was hardly some desperate idiot who'd fall at the feet of a man so handsome it made me want to light myself on fire.

I had self-respect. I had my pride.

But, apparently, my body didn't give two shits about pride. *He's yummy yummy yummy yummy and you should jump on that ASAP. Get down and dirty for once, girl!*

"Let me think about this proposition," said Olivier. "We can reconvene at nine AM tomorrow." He glanced at his watch. "Or today, rather."

"Fine by me." I stood up, and right then, I could feel exhaustion making my bones practically melt. I yawned, blushing at how loud the sound was.

Olivier stood as well. We stared at each other a long moment, and time seemed to stretch like a rubber band. Where most people would look away, Olivier continued to study me, like I was some strange specimen he'd never encountered before. It was unsettling.

I picked up the book of poetry and used it like a shield. "I need to go to bed," I said lamely.

Olivier, though, had placed his arm over my head, caging me in rather effectively against the bookshelf behind me. "Yes, you probably should, *mademoiselle*."

I could feel his heated breath on my face. If someone doused us in water right this second, I was pretty sure it would turn to steam. My heart pounding, I ducked under his arm and headed back to my room without another word. I heard him chuckle at my retreating figure, which only made me hate him more.

CHAPTER SIX

The following morning, I woke up just as the sun was coming up. I never woke up this early, but I had barely been able to sleep last night after my bizarre conversation with Olivier. I was almost halfway convinced I'd dreamed the entire thing. Yet as I rubbed the sleep out of my eyes and put on some pants and a sweater, I knew I hadn't dreamed it at all.

I hurried down to the kitchen. Not just because I desperately needed coffee, but because I needed information. The kitchen was already bustling when I entered. A few people glanced at me, but no one stopped me from coming inside. At this point, the staff knew who I was and either ignored me or occasionally inquired if I needed anything.

I looked for red hair, my stomach sinking when I couldn't find Cara. Instead, Mrs. Walsh stepped out from a walk-in fridge, a hand cocked on her hip. "May I help you, miss?" she said, all crispness.

I had to admit, I was impressed at how perfectly ironed her apron was this early and how tightly she'd rolled her hair into a bun. My own hairline winced in pain just looking at it.

"Is Cara here?" I asked.

"It's her day off." Mrs. Walsh stepped around me, which only served to remind me that I was only in the way. When I didn't leave, she asked, "Is there anything else I can do for you?"

"Um." How did I start? Putting my shoulders back, refusing to act like I was wasting her time, I said, "Do you know an employee here named Olivier?"

Mrs. Walsh frowned. "Olivier? Do you mean Oliver?"

"No, Olivier. The French version, I think."

Mrs. Walsh's nose crinkled. "No, I can't say that there's anyone here who's French. Not all the way out here in the middle of nowhere. Besides, a Frenchman would freeze in these parts. Always complaining about the cold, are they." Based on her tone, she seemed to take those complaints about the damp Irish weather personally.

"He's a landscaper. I met him the first day I arrived," I said. "I think he's new?"

"A landscaper? You must be mistaken, miss. The only landscaper we have is Jamie, who's been here longer even than I have." Mrs. Walsh began to gather ingredients to bake some kind of pastry. She began mixing sugar with some butter, beating the mixture with vigor. "Jamie sometimes hires outside help for the spring and summer months, but they wouldn't be French, or English, for that matter."

I couldn't comment on how common it was for someone from France to go work menial labor in Ireland, but I believed Mrs. Walsh. So that meant that nobody knew who Olivier was…which made me wonder—had he even been hired? Or had he just been posing as a worker to gain access to the estate?

I grabbed something to eat and headed back upstairs after thanking Mrs. Walsh, who kept looking at me with suspicion. I went straight to the library, where I waited for Olivier to arrive.

When it was close to eleven in the morning, I was almost convinced that he'd run off. It was a quarter past eleven when he finally waltzed into the library, looking both rumpled and deliciously handsome, the sunlight pouring from the windows giving him an angelic glow.

"Good morning," he said. He raised a paper cup of coffee to his lips. When he saw me frowning, he added, "Bad night?"

"It's nearly noon," I ground out.

He glanced at a clock on the wall. "It's not yet half past eleven."

"It's barely the morning. You said we'd meet in the morning."

He shrugged and settled into the same chair he'd occupied last night. "I never get up before ten AM if I can help it." He peered closely at me. "You do have rather large bags under your eyes. It must've been a bad night for you. Did the thought of me keep you up all night?"

"The thought of how I'm going to dismember you slowly did," I said sweetly.

Olivier just sipped his coffee. He'd obviously been awake long enough to go into the nearest town to grab coffee, which grated on me. Not that he should've brought me something. No, it meant he hadn't felt like this meeting was very important. That he didn't see *me* as important.

Don't get all weird about him, I said to myself. *He's only trying to bait you.*

"If it makes you feel better," said Olivier smoothly, crossing his legs, "I was awake early to think about the position we've found ourselves in. We both want the same thing. We both most likely have information the other wants."

I nodded. "I think we established all of that last night."

"The thing is, I was led to believe that your grandfather had this clock. That information must've been wrong." Olivier scowled. "Or perhaps it was just old information. Who can know? But I'm at somewhat of a dead end."

My palms were sweaty as I said, "I have documentation that shows that my father, not my grandda, is actually the owner of the clock right now."

Olivier blinked in surprise. "Your father?"

"Yes." I handed over the papers Mr. McDonnell had given me. "But for whatever reason, my father had these sent to the estate here."

Olivier's eyes narrowed. "It's signed Sean Gallagher. That's your grandfather, the name I was given. Is that also your father's name?"

"Yes, kind of. But he never went by it. His full name is Sean Connor Gallagher, but he always went by Connor. As far as I know, he never signed as Sean to avoid confusion with his da. Except in this case."

"I'll be damned. I had the wrong man but the right name all along." He returned the papers to me. "Where is your father? Is he alive?"

"That's where things get dicey. I don't know where my da is. I've actually never met him. I thought he was dead for most of my life, but it was only recently I was informed he was still alive." I could feel nerves making me shaky—with fear? Excitement? Maybe both.

"And your father is the one that has my family's clock." Olivier leaned back heavily in the chair. "And you have no idea where he is." He said something in French that even I could tell was a swear.

"Of course that would be the case. Of course."

"Sorry?"

Olivier was silent for a long moment, which I rather hated, because it gave me a chance to ogle him. In our previous encounters, I'd been so distracted with what he was saying that I hadn't taken in quite how handsome he was. Now, watching him, I felt tingles up and down my spine just from *looking* at him. It was ridiculous.

He had the cheekbones of a model, his eyes a piercing gray. And I was fairly certain his hair was naturally golden. But it was everything put together—the smile, the accent, the eyes, the confidence in the way he moved and spoke—that created a figure that seemed more god than man.

"Why do you want this clock so badly?" I said.

"I told you: it's my family's."

"But why go to all of this trouble? Come all the way here to Ireland, play landscaper, snoop around a library...it must be worth something to you personally. Why?"

Olivier's expression shuttered. "It was my mother's," he said grudgingly. "It means a great deal to her, and she wants it returned."

"What happened to it in the first place?"

"It was stolen from her."

I stared at him. "Stolen? Then how could my da have bought it from an antique dealer?"

Olivier shrugged. "Perhaps the dealer didn't know it had been stolen originally. Perhaps the dealer didn't care about its origins."

When I'd looked over the documents my da had had mailed here, I hadn't found any information on the dealer enclosed, which had been strange.

"Why would you tell me this information?" Olivier scowled at me. "What's your angle?"

Did I have an angle? Well, besides wanting to find my father, I guess I had an angle in that regard. Rolling my eyes, I replied, "My only 'angle' is to find this stupid clock and in doing so, my da. That's it. I told you about this because I thought…" I swallowed, the words drying up in my throat.

I thought what? That we'd team up? Now I realized that spilling the beans about my father maybe hadn't been a great idea. I didn't have much else to bargain with beyond that crucial piece of intel.

Trying to tame the blush that was creeping into my cheeks, I said, "If you want this clock, you're not going to get it without my help."

Olivier laughed. "And how do you figure that, *mademoiselle*?" He looked at his nails, appearing bored. "Now that I know who actually owns this antique, I can leave this damp, Godforsaken country—"

I stood up. "I'm going with you." I pointed a finger in Olivier's face. "I'm going to find my da. Even if it means stowing away in your luggage and stalking you across Europe, I'll do it."

Olivier gently pushed my hand aside. "Pointing is so

gauche. Try to refrain from it." He continued sitting; he gazed up at me, assessing me, I guess. "Then what do you have to offer me?" he said finally.

"Offer you?"

He gestured at me. "What should make me want to bring you along in this search?" He leaned forward now, and he cocked a golden eyebrow. "You're not really my type, but I'm open to an arrangement. You're pretty enough, at least."

Oh, I wanted to slap him. I even raised my hand, palm open, feeling my face turning beet red. "Are you seriously asking me to bargain with sexual favors?"

"If you want to put it that way." He shrugged.

I poked him in the chest. Well, maybe more like *pushed* him, if I were being honest. "I'm not sleeping with you. I have no interest in you whatsoever." *Liar.* "I want to find my da. I've never met him, and I've always wanted to know why he left me and my brother. Why he left our mom when she was dying from cancer." Hurt filled my voice despite my best efforts to tamp it down. "This isn't about some antique, or a grift, or some scheme to get into your most likely gonorrhea-filled pants. I'm going to find my da, and you can either help me, or you can eat a bag of musty dicks."

Olivier pushed my hand away a second time, standing slowly, forcing me to back up if I didn't want our bodies to collide.

Before he could reply, I said, "And if you do find my da, do you really think he's going to sell you the clock in the first place? He sent those documents here because he wanted to prove a point to my grandda. What, I don't know. But I'm going to take a flying leap and say that he's not just going to hand the thing over."

"I'm willing to pay a lot of money. Most people can be convinced if the price is right."

"Maybe. But we're Irish. We're stubborn, and from everything I've heard about my da's side of the family, the stubbornness is legendary." I tipped up my chin. "But if it were me asking for the clock, I would have a better chance. Hell, I could guilt my da into just giving it to me."

Olivier narrowed his eyes. "And what? You'd simply…gift it to me?"

"Yes. If you took me with you on this wild-goose chase."

"I don't know what this has to do with geese."

"It's an expression." I waved a hand. "It doesn't matter. How about it? Do you want to team up and figure this out together?"

Olivier considered me. I nearly squirmed under his scrutiny. He assessed me, rather like how he'd assess a horse he wanted to buy. It wasn't a pleasant feeling.

"I do not know if I can truly trust you," he said slowly, "but perhaps you cannot truly trust me, either."

"I trusted you enough to tell you about my da." *Trusted enough—or was stupid enough*, I thought. *Same difference.*

"Yes, you did. Then perhaps I can be truthful with you. When I said the clock was stolen, that's not entirely true." He pushed his fingers through his hair. "I stole the clock to pay off debts I'd made gambling."

"You stole your mom's beloved antique clock? That's low."

"I thought it was just another antique that had been gathering dust. She'd never mentioned it was important to her or I never would've taken it. She

55

didn't even know it had been missing until a year later."

"Still not a great look there, dude."

He ignored me. "I know who I sold the clock to, but it was five years ago. The clock has obviously been sold a number of times since then." He rubbed his chin.

"Then we could talk to your guy. Follow the bread-crumbs that way," I said.

"I wanted to avoid this, because it will take who knows how long. That's why I came here, but since no one knows where you father is..." His gaze landed back on my face before he put out his long-fingered hand. "If you agree to give me the clock if we find your father, then I'll agree to finance any travel we may do."

I blinked. I hadn't expected that. It seemed too good to be true. "For real?"

Olivier smiled. "For real." His hand still was held out. "Shake?"

I took his hand, the feeling of his fingers against my own nearly electric. Something heated passed between us, even in that brief touch.

"Okay," I said softly. "You have a deal."

"Oh, and one other thing."

"Yes?" I waited breathlessly, feeling my pulse hammering in my throat.

All suavity, Olivier said, "Never use the phrase 'gon-orrhea-filled pants' in my vicinity again."

CHAPTER SEVEN

Three days later, Olivier and I were off to Paris. He'd tried calling this antiques dealer he'd sold his mother's beloved clock to, but the number had been disconnected. Despite our best efforts at Googling contact info, all we had was an address in Paris for a tiny antiques shop that might not even still exist.

Olivier had assured me he'd take care of booking the flights. Although I'd agreed to him financing this trip, I'll admit, I'd expected that it would involve him paying for gas as we traveled to and from Dublin, not flying to fucking Paris! I'd told him that I'd find the money for the flight. The last thing I wanted was to feel like I owed him something.

But before I'd booked my own ticket, Olivier came into the library to tell me, "I booked our tickets."

My face twitched. "*Our?* I told you I'd pay for mine."

He shrugged. "You can pay me back if you want." He looked at his phone. "Five hundred euros."

My jaw dropped. "Jesus Christ, we're just going to Paris! Did you hire a private jet or something?"

"No, of course not. First class will do." He sounded completely serious, too.

And of course, that sum of money would be more in American dollars. I didn't even want to look up the exchange rate. I'd need to ask Liam to send me the money, which meant I'd have to tell him what we were doing…

"Can you cancel my ticket?" Sweat was beading on my forehead at the mere thought of divulging this plan to my older brother. He'd probably show up and haul me back to Washington in a burlap sack.

"Why would I do that? Are you reneging on your promise?"

"No," I ground out. "I just don't want to pay that much for a plane ticket."

His smile was so obnoxious that I was way too tempted to strangle him in the middle of the library. "Then shouldn't you be thanking me?"

"Thank you." I nearly snarled the words.

"*De rien, mademoiselle.*" He even bowed, the dick.

"But I am paying you back. I just can't pay you back right this second." I wanted to swallow my tongue and die right there on the spot, having to admit that. "But I will when I can."

"Suit yourself."

When we arrived at Dublin Airport at the buttcrack of dawn the next day, I couldn't help but notice that Olivier's passport wasn't French. I mean, the language looked like French, but the country on it wasn't one I'd heard of.

"Where are you from, exactly?" I asked him after we'd arrived at our gate.

He gave me a strange look. "France, of course." He said something else in French, just to be annoying.

"Yes, I know you speak French." I rolled my eyes. "But I saw your passport. It wasn't a French one."

"I'm from Salasia," he said finally.

"Oh." I counted to three in my head before asking, "And where is that?"

"Between France and Italy. It's a small principality."

I waited for more information, but he merely sipped his Americano and proceeded to ignore me until we boarded. When we got in line for first class, though, the flight attendant's eyes widened when she looked at his passport.

She rattled something in rapid-fire French. I caught Olivier's name but obviously nothing else. Olivier replied, the flight attendant said something else, and then I yawned loudly, making Olivier say, "Sorry to bore you so."

"But you're so good at it," I said sweetly. I handed my passport to the attendant, whose entire focus remained on Olivier. She was way too excited to see his stupid, handsome face. Then again, he was handsome. Maybe she was just super thirsty for attractive men today.

Olivier and I were in our seats when an elderly couple boarded, the woman using a cane. They stopped at our row, the man saying that we were sitting in their seats.

"I'm so sorry," the flight attendant told Olivier, me, and the elderly couple minutes later. "The flight has been overbooked in first class. We do have two seats in coach, and we'll compensate whoever is willing to move.

Please accept my upmost apologies to you all for the inconvenience."

Olivier looked at me. Then he looked at the elderly woman resting on her cane. "Of course they can have our seats," he said smoothly.

The flight attendant took us nearly to the back of the plane, right next to the engine. Great, they gave us the crappiest seats on the plane.

One person was already sitting in the row in the middle seat. He was a big guy. When he stood up to let me by, his head nearly touched the ceiling of the plane.

I took the window seat; Olivier took the aisle. Big Guy in the middle proceeded to spread his legs as far as he could, take up both armrests, and then promptly fell asleep and started snoring before we'd even gotten into the air.

Olivier made a face when his arm touched Big Guy's arm. I couldn't stop myself from laughing.

"Have you never ridden in coach?" I said.

"Of course I have." Olivier pulled his tray table down, only to make another face when he found it covered in some mysterious, sticky substance.

"Business class doesn't count."

"I don't know the difference." Olivier pressed the call button. A different flight attendant than the one who'd been drooling over him came by. "May I have a menu?"

"We don't serve meals in coach."

I couldn't see Olivier's expression, but I had a feeling it was all surprise. "How is that possible? What kind of plane is this?"

The flight attendant, a no-nonsense Irishwoman,

gave him a bored look. "Lad, you're in coach. You'll get a bag of crisps and be grateful."

I had to cover my mouth to keep from laughing so loudly that I'd wake our snoring neighbor.

"It's not that funny," growled Olivier.

"Oh, oh, oh," was all I could say between snorts and guffaws. "You think you can get meals on coach! You're adorable. What else? Do you think you get free cocktails and a hot towelette?" I nearly peed my pants laughing.

Big Guy's right eye opened to look at me. "Loud," he said.

"Sorry."

He'd already fallen back to sleep.

"I never drink alcohol on flights," groused Olivier. He then attempted to lean his seat back, but since our row was right in front of the restroom, he couldn't. "Are you fucking *serious*—"

Big Guy opened his left eye. "Language!"

Olivier, for once, seemed cowed. "My apologies," he muttered.

I, for one, wasn't going to anger our neighbor. I put my headphones in and started reading, trying my hardest not to glance at Olivier out of the corner of my eye to see if he was going to do anything ridiculous again. Throughout the flight, he kept trying to cross his legs, but there wasn't enough room. At one point, he'd put his feet somewhat into the aisle, only to have some poor sucker trip over them and cause Olivier to yelp in surprise.

I took out my headphones to hear Olivier apologizing, the tripper apologizing, and even the flight attendant behind the tripper apologizing. It was practically an apology orgy.

I glanced up at Big Guy. He was still sound asleep, a line of drool hanging from his mouth. Sometimes he let out a particularly loud snore that was loud enough for me to hear through my headphones, but apparently not loud enough to wake himself up.

I'd dozed off when I was awoken to a woman's voice nearby. She kept getting louder. I yawned, turning off my music, half expecting someone else to be raging at Olivier. But, no, it was the flirty flight attendant from when we'd boarded along with another one.

The second flight attendant was no older than me, but where I was straight as a board and not remotely feminine, she was curvy, blond, and wore blindingly red lipstick that complimented her skin beautifully. Despite being stuck in a cramped plane in dry, recycled air and terrible lighting, she managed to look glowy. I'd be annoyed, if I weren't thoroughly impressed.

"May I get your autograph?" Blond Flight Attendant said, her accent marking her as Irish. "I'm a huge fan," she gushed.

I blinked. She was asking Olivier for an autograph? Why? Just because he was hot?

The French flight attendant who'd spoken with Olivier earlier said in accented English, "Oh, I don't know what I should have you sign—"

From where I was sitting, I could just make out French girl's name badge: Nicole. Nicole was currently searching in her pockets, even going so far as to look down her blouse, as if a notepad would just be waiting in her cleavage to use for this occasion.

"Here, how about I sign this?" Olivier pulled out a journal from his backpack and tore off two pages of what looked like nice paper. "If I'd known you two would be on board, I would've brought something nicer to sign." He winked. Winked!

I made a gagging noise. Olivier shot me a dark look before he returned to autographing.

"Can you make it out to Elsie?" said the blond flight attendant. "That's Elsie with an 'ie' at the end. Oh, and can you sign it as 'Prince'?"

I could only see half of Olivier's face, but I could see his smile falter. "I never sign my name like that," he said, the words rather harsh.

I had to admit, I was watching this with avid interest. Why these women wanted him to sign their autographs like he was some royal prince, I didn't know.

After the women finally went back to work, I leaned so I could catch Olivier's attention. "Hey! What the hell was that all about?"

Olivier shrugged one shoulder. "No idea."

"You're such a liar." I tried to lean closer, but that just meant I was pressing my arm against Big Guy's. I checked to make sure he was still sleeping: he was. "Why did they want you to sign their autographs like that?"

"I'm not discussing this right now."

"Well, where are you gonna go? Hide in the bathroom for the rest of the flight?"

Olivier studiously ignored me after that. But what he didn't know was that, as a younger sister, I'd learned how to annoy my brother until he cried uncle ages ago. I tossed paper balls at Olivier. When that didn't make him look at me, I just kept repeating over and over again, "Hey, Prince. Hey. Prince. Prince. Hey. Prince. Olivier. Prince, Prince, Prince—"

"Will you fucking stop?" Olivier exploded. He nearly

burst from his seat, which resulted in him elbowing Big Guy right in the ribs.

Big Guy's eyes popped open. He stared down at Olivier, like a bear woken from hibernation. He said slowly, "Don't touch."

"Sorry. Not much room back here."

Big Guy's eyes narrowed. "Language," was all he said before he closed his eyes.

"Hey, how about you tell me what that was all about before I wake up our neighbor and get you torn limb from limb?" I said.

Olivier scowled. "You wouldn't."

I showed him my phone. I unplugged my headphones, "W.A.P." about to play as loudly as possible from my phone. My thumb hovered over the play button. "Three, two, one—"

"Fine! Fine!" Olivier glared at me so hard that I could feel my shirt burning up. "Anyone tell you that you're a menace?"

"Every day. Now explain."

Olivier crossed his arms, looking like a little boy who'd been denied a second piece of cake. "What do you want to know?" he said.

"Seriously?" I rolled my eyes. "Why did they want your autograph? What's the prince thing about?"

"It's because I am a prince," he said in a low voice.

"What?"

He shot me a look. "Do I need to repeat myself?"

I just stared at him, my eyes bugging out of my head.

"A prince? What does that even mean—" I cut myself off, mostly because Olivier's glare was so hot that I had a feeling he'd strangle me if I didn't shut up.

I realized that I'd never asked him his last name. When I'd asked him where he was from, he'd been dodgy. I was about to search on my phone, but I refused to pay ten euro for thirty minutes of internet. My curiosity would have to wait until we landed.

Olivier didn't say another word to me the entire flight. When we landed in Paris later that morning, I nearly threw my phone down the plane aisle because it refused to connect to the internet. "Weak signal," it kept telling me. There were no wi-fi signals I could connect to, either.

Big Guy had woken up after the plane had landed. When I swore under my breath at my stupid phone, he tapped me on the shoulder.

"Sorry, language," I said without looking at him.

He tapped me again, a bit harder.

I finally looked up at him. He said in the blandest tone ever, "He's a prince. A real one."

Olivier was currently getting his suitcase from the bin overhead, nearly getting into a fight with a guy who'd reached over him. The two were bickering like schoolchildren at the moment. Great. Just what I needed: Olivier getting arrested before we'd even gotten off of the plane.

"What?" I said to Big Guy.

Big Guy pointed at Olivier. "Prince. He's one." He gave me a pitying look. "You didn't know?"

"Of course I didn't—" I then said to Olivier, "Are you going to duel the guy? It's not that serious!"

Olivier's face was red. "He almost hit me in the head with his bag—"

"If you had moved when I said *excuse me*," the other guy said obnoxiously.

Big Guy, for his part, slowly lifted himself out of his seat and gently pushed the two idiots apart. "No fighting." He gestured at me. "Line is moving. Hurry up."

Olivier looked completely nonplussed, while the other guy had already moved to leave the plane. By the time we were all off, I was about to burst with questions for Olivier. But before I could once again get my phone out to search online, Big Guy beat me to the punch.

He pointed to Olivier. "Be nice to her. Just because you're rich and royalty doesn't make you better." He then turned to me. "He's not that famous of a prince. I only know about him because my mom is obsessed with royals. He won't even be king."

Big Guy waved a goodbye as Olivier and I watched him lumber away.

"We don't even have a king," groused Olivier. "We're a fucking principality."

My head ached. "I'm so confused."

Olivier slung an arm across my shoulders. "You and me both. Let's get out of here and get something to eat. I'm famished."

CHAPTER EIGHT

Olivier finally spilled his guts at lunch. We found a little cafe a few blocks from our hotel—it was too early to check in, so we still had our bags with us—and I was currently stuffing my face with pastries and drinking two lattes in a row.

The city bustled around us: people walking and talking, cars going by, bicycles cycling past. The sound of French being spoken filled the air, although I heard a lot of English and other languages as well. Nearby was a couple sitting on a bench, both of whom were eating what looked like éclairs. Why hadn't I ordered an éclair? I needed to do that ASAP.

I'd practically stuffed my face with food—a delicious chocolate croissant followed by two different flavored éclairs, coffee flowing freely, and then a platter of macarons and petit fours that were so amazing that I nearly cried.

"Are you even listening to me?" Olivier cocked his head to the side.

"What was this again?" I held up a bun filled with some kind of preserves.

"Brioche." His lips twitched. "If you keep eating, you'll make yourself sick. Have you never had French food?"

"Sure, there are some French places in Seattle. But this is Paris. You can't compare the two." I bit into the brioche, tasting lemon preserves along with the yeasty dough. Oh God, I was going to orgasm right here in the middle of the café, and I didn't even care.

As I'd eaten, Olivier had told me the following:

- He was, in fact, a prince.
- His official title was Hereditary Prince of Salasia.
- His full name was Olivier Étienne Jean Louis Valady, Hereditary Prince of Salasia, because he was just that fancy.
- Salasia was a small principality nestled between France and Italy.
- Olivier's father was the current ruler of Salasia.
- His father was the head of state, but it was mostly a title without any real power behind it.
- His father could not order anyone to be guillotined. (You're a royal but can't send anyone to get their head chopped off?)
- The royal family did not have a dungeon where they tortured political rivals. (So Olivier claimed…)
- He really didn't appreciate my joke about his crown jewels.

"Wow," was all I said after he'd given me the rundown. "So does that mean you're rich?"

"What a gauche question." He looked genuinely offended.

"I'm American. We're all gauche." I said this as I popped the last bite of brioche into my mouth and sighed happily.

"I've always heard Americans love to talk about money."

"We do love money, guns, and freedom. I can practically hear a bald eagle soaring overhead as I say that."

Olivier sipped his tea. "If you really want to know, I'm not rich, but I do receive an allowance as a member of the royal family."

"That was a lot of words to say that you're loaded."

He scowled. "I'm not discussing this. It's not relevant."

Considering his "not-rich" state was what was paying for us to travel around Europe, I was skeptical of this claim. But it didn't matter. What mattered was that I was now gallivanting in Paris with a Royal Prince of Salasia. How quaint!

I desperately wanted to text Rachel about all of this. She'd die when I told her. She'd always been obsessed with the British Royal Family. She'd gotten up at the crack of dawn to watch Prince William marry Kate Middleton and had sighed over her wedding dress for way too long.

Honestly, I hadn't understood what all the fuss was about. They were just figureheads. They wielded zero political power. They just had a lot of money and land, and they were hanging onto an obsolete system by the skin of their teeth. What was to admire?

Olivier continued to sip his tea. Never once had he eaten with his mouth open; he'd lay his knife down between individual bites of his meal. He dabbed his lips with his cloth napkin with such finesse that I felt a bit like of an ogre in comparison. I probably could've at least attempted to act civilized, but his expression of amazement/disgust at my eating so much was honestly so hilarious that I hadn't been able to help from trolling him further.

Then he said, "You don't seem impressed."

"With what?" I'd been staring into my empty cup of coffee, wondering if three lattes in a row would kill me.

"With me. With what I told you."

I laughed. "Why should I be impressed? You didn't do anything besides get lucky when you were born."

"True. But most people tend to look upon royals with a bit more awe than you're currently exhibiting."

"I'm an American. We don't care about royals."

Olivier snorted. "Ridiculous. You lot are way more obsessed with the British royals than anyone in Britain."

Okay, he had me there. "Well, if you want me to scrape and bow and drool over you, you're going to be disappointed."

"I never asked for drooling." His tone was wry. He fell silent again, studying me. I felt a bit like a bug under a microscope.

Had he really never met someone who didn't care about his title? "Is there something on my face?" I said finally.

"No," was all he said.

But his gray eyes didn't leave my face for way too long. It was to the point that I muttered about going to the bathroom and hurried away. My heart was pounding my chest, my cheeks flushed.

Why did this handsome jerkface get me so flustered? After peeing, I washed my hands with vigor. "Don't let him intimidate you," I said to myself. I splashed some cold water on my cheeks. The last thing I needed was Olivier to see that I was blushing like a teenage girl.

On my way back to our table, a woman stopped me, speaking in French.

"Oh, I'm sorry, I don't speak French."

She switched to accented English effortlessly. "Are you dating Prince Olivier?"

I looked over at Olivier, and there was already a small crowd around him, all of whom were young women. Oh, great.

"Um, no," I said. "We're just..." My brain tried to scramble for some reasonable explanation. "Working together."

"Oh, that makes more sense," she said. She hurried off to catch Olivier's attention before I could say something snarky.

I returned to the table, and I had to almost elbow the young women out of the way just to get my suitcase and bag. I rolled my eyes at Olivier. "Seriously?" I said.

He was standing already and ignored my remark. The girls spoke to him in French, and as I couldn't understand anything any of them say, I place some euros down and headed outside to wait for him.

I was tapping my foot with impatience when he finally joined me. I glared at him. "Seriously?" I repeated.

"Do you have a question?" was his overly calm rejoinder.

Okay, I didn't. I was just annoyed at that woman thinking there was no way Olivier would ever date me. Because of course I wanted him to want to date me, even though I didn't want to date him. Yeah, made sense. *Niamh, you dingus.*

"It's nothing," I said in irritation. "Let's go check into the hotel."

"You seem annoyed."

The sun was way too hot right now. I could feel lower back getting damp, beads of sweat forming on my upper lip. I wiped at the moisture. God, the last thing I needed was to get pit stains right now.

"I'm not annoyed," I replied.

"You sound annoyed."

"I do not."

"You sound as though seeing all those women surround me made you unhappy."

Oh, he was needling me, all right. I gritted my teeth. "If you want to know, my stomach hurts from eating so much. It has nothing to do with you."

"Hmm."

I glanced up at him, even more irritated to see that he seemed incapable of sweating despite the heat and dragging his suitcase behind him. His shirt collar was open, exposing golden skin. His clavicle looked so lickable that I nearly tripped over a sidewalk crack thinking about it.

"I don't care if you don't believe me," I said, my voice taut. "That's your issue, not mine."

"Do you know what your issue is? You're so determined to seem like you don't care about me that you become..." He paused. "What is the word?"

"I have no idea," I said, deadpan.

Olivier said, "Sanctimonious. That's the word."

My jaw dropped. "Sanctimonious? The hell I am."

"I knew disclosing my identity to you would make things awkward." He sounded genuinely frustrated. "You now find me intimidating, but instead of admitting as much, you're now lashing out at me."

Good lord, I did not need this psychobabble, no matter how accurate it might be. Stopping, I turned to look him in the face. "I don't find you intimidating. What I find *annoying* is that we keep getting delayed in our objective because you constantly have groupies coming around to ask for your autograph like you're Harry Styles or something."

"Who?"

"One Direction? Never mind. It's not important." We'd finally arrived at the hotel, thank God. I was sweating like crazy, and I was probably bright red from the exertion. Although I didn't have red hair, I did have the complexion of a redhead. I blamed my da for that one.

When we checked in, the man at the front desk spoke just to Olivier while I waited. It was only when we went to the elevator and I asked for my key that Olivier said, "We're in the same room."

"What? We agreed to separate rooms."

"They only booked us for one, and there isn't another one available." Olivier handed me a second key. When I didn't take it, he added, "There are two beds, sweetheart. I promise not to compromise you."

I took the key with a low growl. "Fine. Great. We'll stay in the same room."

Because my life was apparently one big joke, when

we opened our door, I saw a grand total of one bed. It was a king-sized bed, but still.

"I'll call for a rollaway bed," I said.

He lifted one eyebrow. "The bed is big enough for three people. We can share."

I really, really did not want to share a bed with this arrogant prince, and I really, really, did not want admit it was because a part of me want to grab him and ravish him. He said I wouldn't have to worry about him getting handsy? Joke was on him, because apparently, I was the one lacking in self-control.

When I sat down on the bed, I had to admit, it was comfortable. The thought of having to sleep on a hard rollaway bed did not interest me. I waited for Olivier to play the gallant prince and volunteer to sleep on the roll-away, but no. He merely placed his suitcase on top of the one stand we had and said that he was going to shower.

I was listening to the water run as I considered my options. Mostly, though, I was just tired. Even though it was early afternoon, I felt like I could sleep for an entire day. What was it about flying and traveling that was so exhausting when you were just sitting for hours upon end? I slipped off my tennis shoes and curled up on the bed, falling asleep before Olivier had even finished his shower.

～

I AWOKE around five PM to find a note left on the table next to me.

I went for a walk. Text me if you need to.

-O

I rubbed the sleep from my eyes. I felt even sleepier than before I'd closed my eyes. Ugh, this was why I didn't take naps. I sniffed my armpits, only to grimace when I inhaled. Yeesh, I needed to take a shower.

Standing under the hot water, I sighed happily. I scrubbed the grit of the plane and the sweat that had dried from my body. I was mostly awake by the time I got out of the shower. I wiped the condensation from the mirror and considered my reflection, thinking about that Frenchwoman at the cafe who thought it so strange that Olivier would want to date me.

I wasn't the type of girl to think of myself as super uggo. I'd had my fair share of men who'd been interested in me. Not that my beauty was based on how men saw me, but I wasn't a girl who just had no idea how she looked to other people. I'd always liked my hair—dark and full—and my nose was nice. My lips were full.

My eyes were a nice color, but despite my dark hair, my eyelashes weren't rather pale. I had a bunch of new freckles on my nose and chest, and seeing them, I smiled. I didn't wear makeup very often, and I always preferred to make sure my freckles were visible if I did. I never understood why people wanted to cover them up. They were cute, like sprinkles tossed across my skin.

But I was hardly a supermodel. It had never bothered me. I'd always preferred wearing jeans and tennis shoes and working on cars. I'd never cared much about my appearance. What had it gotten me? Not much. I preferred people to want me around for my brain or my skills, anyway.

Yet those words from earlier prickled across my skin like little needles. I suddenly felt self-conscious about being on the itty-bitty titty committee (I'd pretty much been its president my entire lift) or the fact that my teeth weren't perfectly straight. My teenage self had balked at how nerdy braces looked, but now my adult self hated that I'd been so self-conscious.

I shook my head. I finished toweling off, feeling extremely silly. Even if Olivier was interested in me, it wasn't like anything could come of it. He was a prince, for God's sake. He was going to inherit a literal throne. Did I want the scrutiny that came with that life?

The mere thought of that sort of life made me chuckle under my breath. Yeah, that was about as likely as my boobs turning in to DDDs. Not gonna happen.

I emerged from the bathroom in a robe, only to see that Olivier still hadn't returned. But since I was still hot from my shower, the robe made me even warmer. I tossed it back into the bathroom and walked nude to my suitcase, my back to the hotel room door.

I was digging around for a fresh pair of panties when I heard the click of the lock. I stood up straight the moment Olivier came inside to see me holding a too-short t-shirt to my naked body.

"Well, this is a pleasant sight," he said in amusement.

I squawked. I threw my shirt at him, which was stupid because I was now completely uncovered. "Get out of here!" I grabbed the comforter from the bed, but it was tucked in so tightly that I could only get a corner of it free. I wrapped it around my waist, my arm across my breasts. "What are you still doing here?" I demanded.

"Just enjoying the spectacle." He sat down in a chair. "You Americans are so finnicky about nudity."

"This isn't the time to talk about our cultural differences. Get. Out!"

He instead covered his eyes with his hand, sighing heavily. "My eyes are closed. Go about your business."

I waved a hand in front of his face: no reaction. Scowling, I dressed quickly, my face on fire.

Honestly, I wasn't that much of a prude or that self-conscious. But having Olivier peruse my body like that had been just beyond embarrassing, especially if he hadn't been impressed at what he'd seen. Oh God, I wanted to die.

I grabbed my key card and wallet, putting on my shoes. "I'm done," I said. "I'm going to go get something to eat."

Before I could run to the ends of the earth, Olivier rose and gently pushed a tendril of damp hair behind my ear. "You're red as a beet."

That made me even redder. "Thanks for pointing that out," I said acidly.

He let his fingers brush against my cheek. He was smiling. "So prickly. Don't be embarrassed."

"I'm not," I lied.

He took my chin in between my fingers, the touch electric. I froze in his grasp. "Shame you hide that body of yours under those clothes," he mused.

At that lovely non-compliment, I reared backward. "Wow, thanks. Anyone ever tell you that you're the least charming prince ever?"

He didn't seem the least bit ruffled. "Oh no, Niamh, believe me, you're the first and only. For so many reasons."

I fled from the room before I could ask him what, exactly, that even met.

CHAPTER NINE

"I think it might be closed," I said.

"The windows are boarded up. Of course it's closed." Olivier, for his part, kept trying to peer through the small spaces between the wooden boards hammered to the windows. Like he'd be able to see someone inside. But he was so agitated, I wasn't about to tell him as much.

"Shit," said Olivier. "Shit, shit, shit."

I yawned. "Yeah, pretty much."

We'd taken a taxi across Paris to find this antiques shop, the address of which Olivier had on a small piece of paper in his pocket. Despite both of our attempts to find the address on Google Maps, Google kept trying to redirect us to some random spot that turned out to be a broken-down bridge on the Seine.

So we'd had to wander around on foot. Olivier had stopped to ask for directions—which made me grateful that he spoke French, but I wouldn't tell him that, no way—but we got a lot of confused expressions. One man told us we were in the wrong part of Paris entirely.

Another woman said that we were in the right area but the wrong street.

"Why are the streets here so confusing?" I'd said multiple times.

"Paris is an old city." He gave me a look that screamed *duh.*

"Well, yeah. But that doesn't mean that they couldn't have made it slightly less confusing in the last century."

Olivier snorted. "Have you ever met a Frenchman?"

I'd always thought that was Seattle, with its five-way intersections and random one-way streets was stressful. Paris, though, was a billion times worse.

And by the time we'd found this antiques shop, luck would have it that the shop was no longer a shop. It was just a boarded-up building with some graffiti sprayed across it.

"Are you sure this is the right place?" I asked.

"Yes. Look." He pointed to a torn awning. He pulled away the cloth to reveal a sign that was barely legible, it was so covered in graffiti. But under the paint, I could make out the store name, Antiquités Durand.

We stood there for a long moment, both of us silently wondering what the hell we were going to do next.

"I'd ask you what we should do next," I said, "but based on the constipated look on your face, you have no idea."

Olivier gave me a look of disgust. "I do not have a constipated face."

I sipped my latte. "If you say so."

Okay, I was needling him, because I was still embarrassed by him seeing me naked yesterday evening. He hadn't stopped ribbing me about it until we'd gone to sleep. At that point, I'd threatened to murder him by strangulation with the shower curtain if he wouldn't shut up.

Oh, and he'd slept on the rollaway bed. I'd forced him after I'd guilt-tripped him for walking in on me naked. He'd whined and moaned about it all morning, accusing me of breaking his back, the big baby.

"We could ask people who work around here. Maybe they know where the guy went," I said.

"That's the smartest idea I've heard from you since we arrived."

I flipped him the bird. He just laughed at me.

Despite my smart idea, I couldn't be of much use in talking to people. Although most people spoke English, Olivier seemed to get more information easily by speaking French. It made sense. Besides, having some random American girl ask you questions about where some antiques owner had gone would seem extra weird. Not that every single French person hated Americans. It was more the overall oddness of it that made people less likely to give out information.

Two hours later, Olivier came outside to where I was waiting for him. "I got it," he said, triumphant. "He's dead."

"You're happy that this guy is dead? Geez, Olivier, how gauche of you."

He ignored me. "No, I meant that I received information about where his widow is located." He showed me a piece of paper with crabbed writing on it.

"Somebody just gave up her location?"

"It's a phone number, not an address."

I peered more closely at the handwriting. It looked

like Greek to me. "Okay, so you're just going to call this woman and say...what?"

Olivier shrugged. "A version of what I've been telling everyone today, that I'm on the quest to find my dying mother's beloved antique clock and that if they can provide me with any information it would be of the greatest importance."

"Your mother is dying?" Now I felt badly for needling him.

At that, he looked away. "Um, well. Not exactly."

"You're guilting people into helping you by saying your mom is dying?" I gaped at him, and then I made the sign of the cross across my chest. "You need Jesus. There's a church down the street. You should go in there and confess your sins."

"It will only result in me telling the priest all about how I saw your naked breasts yesterday—"

I slapped a hand over his mouth. He retaliated by licking my palm. I squawked like an enraged chicken.

"I hope you get eaten by a flock of rabid pigeons!" was my intelligent rejoinder as I stalked off.

"We don't have rabies here in Europe."

Oh my God, who fucking cared! Beyond irritated, I kept walking with no destination in mind. We were too far from the hotel to walk back, though, so I eventually had to either give up my huffing and puffing or call a taxi for myself.

"You seem particularly enraged that I saw you naked," he said when he'd caught up with me. "You Americans are so strange about nudity."

I tossed my latte in the trash, but I missed and nearly hit an actual pigeon instead. The flock of them burst into flight, yelling at the indignity.

"Try not to murder any wildlife while we're here." Olivier picked up my latte and threw it into the bin.

I sighed. "Thank you," I said grudgingly.

"Mademoiselle." He sketched me a bow.

We continued walking. "You never answered my question," he said.

"Was there a question?"

"Perhaps not. But why are you so embarrassed?"

God, he was like a dog with a bone. "Because I don't know you, and it was awkward, and I don't go around flashing my boobs at people, okay?"

"You really should. They're lovely."

I blushed scarlet. "Oh my God—"

"You should go to a nude beach someday." He winked at me. "I think you'd enjoy it after you overcame your initial awkwardness."

With any other guy, I would've told him to go to hell. With Olivier, I was stupidly flattered. Yeah, I was self-conscious about my small boobs, so sue me. Having him tell me he liked them was an ego boost I hadn't realized I'd wanted or needed.

Have a prince compliment my tits—check.

"Um, thanks? Again?" I tucked a stray tendril of hair behind my ear. "It's not that I'm embarrassed by nudity in general. I just don't feel the need to show everybody the goods, you know? And yeah, maybe it is some American prudishness in there, too. It's just not something that's common."

I wrinkled my nose in memory. "Well, except for the nude bicyclist that rides around in Seattle. Which just sounds like a great way to get your balls smashed against the seat, yikes."

"What a lovely mental image."

"Hey, you were the one who brought up the whole nudity subject." Silence fell between us. For a moment, I considered letting it continue, but pettiness overruled logic. "Are you showing off your goods to anyone recently?"

Olivier gave me an amused look. "Are you inquiring if I'm sleeping with someone?"

"Yeah, I guess."

"I had no idea you cared." That came out like a purr.

I nearly tripped over a sidewalk crack again. Geez, I seriously pathetic. "Turnabout is fair play. You have to tell me something embarrassing about yourself since you saw my tits."

"Is that a rule somewhere?"

"It is. It's my rule."

He chuckled. Tilting his head back, he basked in the warm sunlight. He looked like a cat that had found a sunbeam to absorb. And because he was apparently inhuman, he had managed to avoid getting any kind of sunburn. I could make out a light tan deepening his skin color, whereas I'd slathered myself with sunscreen this morning and just prayed that it held up. Such was the downside to my half-Irishness.

"The last woman I dated left me for another man," he said. At my wide-eyed look of surprise, he said rather cuttingly, "Surprised?"

"Surprised that a woman would cheat on a prince? Yeah, kinda."

"The prince part attracts women—and men. That's the simple part. It's all of the baggage that comes with the title that makes women run away in the end."

I hadn't even considered that, if I was being honest.

As the heir to a literal throne, Olivier had more responsibility and scrutiny than I could ever imagine.

"That sucks," I said, rather lamely.

He shrugged. "It's expected. Besides, my parents want me to marry the right kind of girl within the next year. Now that I'm twenty-five, my mother especially wants me to settle down with a good girl and make heirs."

"Twenty-five is hardly old."

He slanted me a look. "I realize that."

I kicked a pebble across the road. "So are you going to marry some princess?"

"Given that Europe's royal families have allowed royals to marry commoners, especially within the last twenty years, no. A princess isn't a requirement. She must be suitable, though. From a good family, with good standing. She must be beautiful, of course."

I rolled my eyes. "Of course. Can't have an ugly princess."

"I sense your sarcasm, but I'm choosing to ignore it." Despite the lightness of his words, I could feel something weighing on him.

And because I'm an idiot, I couldn't help but pry. "Do your parents have someone picked out already?"

"Oh, they have a few." Olivier waved a hand. "One is going to inherit her father's fortune; the other is the daughter of a grand duke of Luxembourg or something as small as Salasia. All very nice women."

"Why do they sound like they're the literal worst, then?"

He grimaced. "They're fine."

"'Fine' is a four-letter word, my dude."

"A marriage with either of them would be acceptable." He stopped to pluck a wildflower from a tiny garden alongside the street. He twirled it between his fingers.

"Acceptable? Don't you want to marry for love?"

The flower stopped twirling. "People like me don't marry for love." He let the flower fall to the ground, but when he turned away, I picked it back up and placed it in my pocket.

What? I was sentimental, okay?

On our way back to our hotel, I stewed over what Olivier had told me. Although a part of me struggled to feel too much sympathy for a man who was rich and handsome and was born into privilege, the other part of me pitied him. He was born into this life, but he hadn't chosen it, either. If he'd been born a regular person, what would he have become? Would he have married for love, gotten a decent job, traveled when they had money, and had lived a normal, boring life?

Most of all, it reminded me that my blossoming infatuation for him could go nowhere. His parents would never approve of me, a nobody Irish-American who hadn't worn a dress since junior high homecoming. I wasn't ashamed of any of those facets of my life, either.

It merely meant that I would be unsuitable for Olivier, and vice versa.

Even as I told myself that, it still stung. Maybe because I was stubborn, but I almost wanted to prove his parents wrong. Which was stupid, because Olivier only liked my boobs and not much else. Hardly a great start to a legitimate relationship.

Who said anything about marriage? my brain said coyly. *Sleep with the guy and get him out of your system. He's clearly attracted to you. And you can go back to America and tell everyone you had sex with an actual prince.*

I hadn't had sex in way too long. Clearly, I was just horny and desperate. But then my mind decided to fill it with all kinds of lurid images—Olivier cupping my breasts, Olivier pulling my jeans down to my ankles as he parted my legs, Olivier pressing a finger inside my pussy—and I had to squeeze my legs together to keep from getting seriously aroused.

I considered seeing if I could get Olivier into bed tonight, but I realized early on that he was too distracted with getting ahold of the antiques' dealer's widow. He called her in the taxi on the way back to our hotel, but no one had picked up, and there'd been no voicemail. Throughout the evening, Olivier had kept calling, despite me telling him that his constant calls would only deter someone from calling him back.

"She's going to block your number," I said for what felt like the thousandth time.

Olivier growled, glaring at his phone. Then he saw my phone in my hand and said, "We'll call from yours."

"Yes, I'm sure she'll be more inclined to answer from a Washington State number." But I handed over my phone regardless. I just hoped it didn't cost me a million dollars in roaming fees.

Olivier tried on my phone twice before calling it a night. As we lay in our respective beds that night, he said, "If we can't find this woman, I don't know where else to go."

I'd thought the same thing. Turning over, I said, "We'll call her from the hotel phone. Then a pay phone. And if all else fails, we'll go back to the store where you got the number to make sure it's right."

He sighed. "Then what? If that doesn't work?"

"Now you're just being a Debbie Downer. We'll figure something out."

"I don't know what a Debbie Downer is."

"It's an expression. It's somebody who's always seeing the glass as half empty."

His expression was wry. "Sometimes the glass is just that: half empty."

I put in my headphones. "Good night, Prince Olivier. Tomorrow is another day."

I didn't hear what he said in reply.

CHAPTER TEN

"He says it's the right phone number," said Olivier in exasperation. He returned to speaking French with the shopkeeper, a middle-aged man with his hair parted right down the middle and smoothed down with an excessive amount of hair gel.

We'd returned to the bookshop where Olivier had gotten the phone number yesterday. Apparently, the shop owner was insisting that the number was correct. I could see Olivier getting frustrated, mostly that the man didn't seem inclined to double-check.

I began to wander through the aisles of books. Most of them were in French, obviously, but I found the small section of English books. Most of the selection consisted of French authors translated into English, along with various classics. At the bottom of the shelf, though, were a handful of romance novels—in English, no less.

I pulled out a historical romance by a favorite author of mine. I hadn't read this one, and I'd already finished the one romance I'd brought with me. I was a total bore and preferred to read printed books still. Probably because they smelled nice. If e-readers could let out a puff of new-book scent, though, I'd buy one in a heartbeat.

"*The Seduction of Miss Emily Morris*," Olivier read over my shoulder. "That rather gives the plot away, no?"

I laughed. "Romance novels aren't known for being subtle."

He plucked the book from my fingers before I could react. He held it over my head as he flipped through it. "Where are the love scenes? Ah, found one." He raised one golden eyebrow as he began to read aloud: "'A fire lit in her belly. Damian's hands were magic. Everywhere he touched, it was like fire across her skin.'"

"Oh my God, stop—"

He just held the book up higher. Tall people were the worst.

"'My nipples beaded and my core moistened,'" he continued. He wrinkled his nose. "Core? Why does this sound like she's describing the earth's core? Is this poor woman full of lava?"

"It's a metaphor." I finally was able to snatch the book from his sneaky, princely fingers. "And yes, it's ridiculously flowery. That's why I like it."

"I'm surprised."

"That I read?"

"No. That you read books like these."

At that, my hackles rose. I had a bit of a love-hate relationship with romance novels. Sometimes they could be so amazing that my mind was blown. But when they were bad, well, they were *bad*. Since I'd been reading them for many years now, I felt like I could criticize them fairly. But when someone—especially a man—

talked derisively about romance novels, I always got defensive.

I could call them trash, but nobody else could.

"Do you want me to hit you upside the head again?" I held up the book. "Because I will if you keep going with that subject."

Olivier jumped back. "Christ, woman. I simply meant that I'm surprised someone as bloodthirsty as you would read romance."

I deflated. "Oh."

"Yes. 'Oh.'" He gestured at me. "Let's go."

To my surprise, Olivier paid for my book, despite my protestations. Maybe he was just trying to ensure that I didn't smack him with it. Well, I wouldn't promise anything.

We began to walk west toward the 7th District where the antiques shop was located. Considering that the Eiffel Tower and other famous landmarks of the city were located in this district, we were quickly walking amongst both Parisians and tons of tourists.

More than once I was asked by an American to help them take a photo. I had no idea how Americans always managed to find each other for photos in foreign countries, but we did.

"So did you have any luck with that phone number?" I said to Olivier.

Olivier sighed. "He insisted it was correct." He pulled the piece of paper from his pocket. "All we can do is keep calling."

I was about to once again ask, *Then what?* But Olivier's expression looked so defeated that I bit my tongue.

It wasn't that I wasn't frustrated at our getting stalled. I wanted to find my da as much as Olivier wanted to find this clock. We both had stakes in this game. The fact that we seemed incapable of finding the one person who'd seemed like a sure thing was beyond annoying.

We walked past the boarded-up antiques shop. Olivier stopped in front of it, frowning.

"What?" I had no idea what was inside that handsome brain of his.

"Do we know who owns this building?"

"Um, no. How would we find that out?"

Olivier stepped back and gazed upward. The building was three stories, and above the abandoned store was a row of windows that looked like offices. Above that, I could see a cat in a window, so most likely they were apartments.

"We need to get inside somehow." He stroked his chin and began to wander to back side of the building. But the only door that led inside was locked. Olivier tried pounding on it, but no one answered. Since no one currently occupied the first floor, it made sense.

We returned to the front of the building once again. Pedestrians flowed past us. A few were annoyed that we were standing in the middle of the sidewalk like two gawking tourists. Except we were gawking at an abandoned store.

I looked up and down the street for some kind of clue. "Wait!" I grabbed Olivier's hand and took him back to the alley behind the building. He grumbled at me until I pointed and said, "Look!"

"It's a window. Unless you want us to break in——"

"No, look. It's open."

Olivier peered more closely. The window itself was small, the glass foggy with age. "Only a crack."

"If we can find something to wedge it open——" I looked around, finding what looked like a piece of pipe that'd fallen out of the nearby trash bins. I began to press the pipe into the crack and slowly making a see-saw motion to get the window to go up.

At first, nothing happened. I kept going, hoping against hope that I wasn't making myself look like an idiot with no results. A moment later, though, Olivier took over and added his strength to wedging the window open. Finally, we heard a creak and the window moved upward.

"Yes!" I pushed it open as far as it would go. Unfortunately, it was just big enough to let one small person through. Meaning, there was no way Olivier was going to get his princely ass through it.

"Hoist me up?" I said.

"And then what? You go upstairs and ask someone to give you a phone number?"

I wrinkled my nose. "No, dingus. I open the door to stairwell so you can do it. Duh."

"I don't think 'dingus' is a real word."

"It totally is. Now, hoist me up already."

Olivier sighed but finally kneeled at my feet, which was just about the greatest image ever. A prince, kneeling at my feet? Come on.

"If this were any other day, I'd totally swoon at having a prince on one knee in front of me," I said, a hand over my heart.

He rolled his eyes. "Stop wasting time already. My trousers are getting dirty."

I laughed at him, but then I was standing on his knee as he boosted me through the window that was about six feet off of the ground. I wiggled through, fearing for a second that my butt was too big to get through. When my hips got stuck, I made a rather absurd squealing noise.

"Are you stuck?" said Olivier. He sounded like he was laughing, the bastard.

I kicked my legs. "Yes! Help me!"

"You're very demanding." Then I felt hands on my thighs, way too close to my butt cheeks, and I couldn't help but clench up. It was almost erotic…until Olivier pushed me through the window and I nearly broke my face as I fell.

Thankfully, I fell on a bunch of old blankets. "Probably shouldn't have gone in headfirst," I muttered to myself. I sneezed, dust motes flowing around me.

"Are you all right?" Olivier called.

"Yeah." I sneezed again. "It's really dusty in here." Which was a sign that this guy who Olivier had sold the clock to had vacated this place a while ago.

The shop—what was left of it—was covered in fabric on the little bit of furniture left over. With little light coming in through the windows, it took me a second to get to the door that opened to the stairwell. It was a different one from the one that led outside. The stairs themselves were clearly very old, and I had to admit, I much preferred Olivier going up them than me doing it.

I opened the door to outside to find Olivier waiting for me. He took in my appearance and said, "You look terrible."

"Wow, thanks."

"No, I mean—" He brushed his thumb across my cheek, making me freeze in shock. "You're covered in dirt."

"That's what happens when you land face-first into a bunch of dusty blankets."

I did my best to clean up my appearance, but apparently, I looked so ridiculous that Olivier thought I'd attract too much attention upstairs.

"We don't want people to think we've broken in. You look just like someone who's snuck inside," he said.

I didn't have a mirror, but based on the amount of dirt and dust on my clothes, I had to reluctantly agree. "Go, go," I said, shooing him. "Before we get caught and get thrown in the Bastille."

Olivier headed upstairs, and I watched his nice ass flex until he turned a corner on the rickety staircase. I hoped he could charm whoever worked up there into giving him the information we needed. If he failed, we were back to square one.

Taking out my phone and turning on the flashlight, I returned to the abandoned store. There were hand-written signs in French scattered about the floor with prices on them. There were a handful of chipped bowls on one table that had seen better days. When I heard something scurry across the floor, I froze in my tracks, half-expecting a giant rat to lunge at my face.

But no rat materialized. Sighing, I kept exploring, drawing my finger through the thick dust, wondering how long it had been since someone had been inside here.

As I wandered, I found a tiny hallway near the west side of the store. A door was ajar, and inside I found what looked like an office. Except there was nothing but a rickety chair and a keyboard that was probably older than I was. On the opposite wall stood a metal file cabinet.

I started opening the cabinet drawers, but there was nothing but empty file folders in the top one. The second: the same. But when I reached the third one, I found a stray envelope that had gotten wedged between the folders and the drawer itself.

I felt a little guilty opening the envelope, but what choice did we have? Besides, I had to do whatever I could to find my da. When I unfolded the three documents, I scanned it, my heart beginning to pound.

It was an insurance document. And on the last piece of paper was an address with the name of the dead man we were searching for: Charles Durand, owner of Antiquités Durand.

An address. We had an address. I nearly tripped over my own feet as I burst from the office, heading for the stairway door.

But then I heard loud voices outside, and straining to hear, I could make out what sounded like Olivier yelling.

I ran outside, wishing I looked less dirty and rumpled, making certain to stuff the envelope into my back pocket.

A dark-haired man was standing with his arms crossed as Olivier spoke. The man just shook his head and replied with what sounded like a negative.

When I came through the alley, the man gave me one look and scowled. He turned back to Olivier, his voice rising. I was pretty sure I heard a word that sounded like "police." Great. That was the last thing we needed.

"Who is this man, honey?" I laced my arm with Olivier's, clinging to him like a vine. "Why is he yelling at you?"

"He's accusing me of breaking and entering," said Olivier with a sniff. "I assured him he was mistaken."

The man's accent was thick as he said to me, "You are very dirty. What were you doing?"

I sniffled, my chin even quivering. "I fell. Look at my hands." I showed him my skinned palms. "My husband would never do something like you're accusing him of. An employee allowed him inside to speak to someone upstairs."

The man's gaze went from me to Olivier and back again. He looked skeptical now.

When I managed to eke out a tear, the man took a step back. "Apologies, madam. I was wrong." He shot Olivier a dark look, but then he scurried back to wherever he came from.

Olivier let out a long sigh. "That was smart thinking," he said, sounding genuinely surprised.

"I have my moments." I wanted to show him the envelope, but not right this second. "Let's go before that guy really does call the cops on us."

We managed to find a bench to sit on in the Champ de Mars, the famous park you could view from the top of the Eiffel Tower. The sun was warm enough that I fanned myself with a pamphlet a vendor had given me. Groups of people sat on the perfectly manicured lawns, some picnicking, others simply catching up on their tans.

Olivier looked grim. "I didn't have an opportunity to speak to anyone. That man you saw me with was instantly suspicious and almost threw me out of the building."

I was giddy with excitement. Pulling the envelope from my pocket, I handed it to Olivier. "Look what I found, though."

Olivier took out the papers, scanning the text. His eyebrows shot to his hairline. "Clever girl," he muttered. He added something in French that I chose to take as a compliment.

"We have no way to know if his widow still lives there," I said, "but at least it's a place to start."

The address itself was still within Paris, although about ten miles from where we were sitting. As Olivier and I looked at the building's facade on Google Maps, I nearly squealed, I was so pleased.

Eventually, Olivier said, "Am I playing your husband now?"

At the reminder, I wrinkled my nose. "It was spur of the moment."

"We're fortunate that man didn't look at your bare finger."

Good point. I should've gone with boyfriend. Why had I chosen husband? I was all of twenty-two. I wasn't exactly ready for marriage, nor was I so thirsty for this golden prince sitting next to me that I wanted to marry him right this second.

Except, as Olivier gazed down at me, his gray eyes inscrutable, I had a feeling I was lying to myself, at least in part. No, I didn't want to marry the guy. But I already knew I wanted to be more than his reluctant ally in this ridiculous quest we were on.

Then he reached out and brushed his thumb against my cheek. His thumb continued its path until it brushed against my lower lip. I began to tremble.

He leaned forward, and I waited for the kiss that never came.

"You still have dirt on your face," he said gruffly, pulling away.

I couldn't breathe. Then a hot blush crept up my face, and I felt very, very stupid for thinking he'd actually wanted to kiss me, right here in the middle of a park.

At that moment, a handful of young women made their way over to Olivier, stars in their eyes. Great. Groupies.

They squealed something in French, and before I knew it, Olivier was standing to meet them, a smile plastered on his face. He spoke to them with enthusiasm, and I swore they all sighed collectively as a single entity.

Feeling petty, I sidled up to him and, like I had earlier in the day, weaved my arm through his. "Baby, who are these women?" I said in a voice that got more strident with every syllable. "You told me you wouldn't cheat on me again!"

The girls looked nonplussed. "Who is this?" one said.

Olivier tried to dislodge my hand, but I just gripped him tighter. "You can't leave me!" I gripped his shirt with my free hand. "I'm pregnant with your baby!"

The girls gaped at Olivier. Olivier, for his part, pushed me rather hard behind him, saying in English, "She's insane. Don't listen to her."

"That's not what you said last night!" I yelled into his back.

It took five more seconds for the girls to turn tail and run. One looked over shoulder and shook her head at us.

Olivier glowered down at me. "Are you happy?" he growled.

"With my baby daddy cheating on me? I'm devastated."

"You're insane. And now those girls are going to post all about this on social media—"

"I'm sure there have been worse rumors about you floating around on the Internet." I patted his arm. "At least I didn't accuse you of murdering puppies."

CHAPTER ELEVEN

My brother Liam glowered at me through my phone screen. "Why do you keep ignoring my calls?" he demanded.

Okay, I had been ignoring his calls. I'd also had yet to inform Liam about the whole thing with Olivier, the clock, and our da. Liam knew I'd gone to Ireland to deal with our grandda's estate, but I hadn't told him I'd wanted to look for our da. He'd blow a gasket.

"I'm busy," I said, which was true. "Besides, the time difference means you keep trying to call me in the middle of the night."

"Not true. I've always called you in the morning here, which would be the afternoon your time." He peered at me, like he could make out all of my secrets. "You look tired."

"Wow, thanks, bro. You always know how to make a girl feel good."

"I told you I didn't want you going over there by yourself. Is it too much? Maybe you should come home." He upped the guilt trip by adding, "Your nieces miss you."

Liam and his wife Mari had two daughters. Fiona had just turned four, while Dahlia was almost two. They were both hellions, and I missed them terribly.

I heard something that sounded like a crash in the background. "Are they setting the house on fire?" I asked.

Liam turned his head to yell, "Leave your mother's makeup alone!" He turned back to me. "She'll rip me limb from limb if they destroy her makeup again."

"Maybe you should go make sure they aren't ruining your marriage and end this call with me."

He laughed darkly. "You wish." He got up, and I got to experience walking with him, which made me a little seasick. I waited for him to deal with my nieces, who'd apparently gotten into one of Mari's expensive eyeshadow palettes but had yet to start using it.

"What did I tell you, Fi?" Liam's voice was frustrated, but I could hear amusement in it, too. "You can't keep using your little sister like a baby doll to practice makeup."

"Aw, Daddy, please!"

You'd have to have a heart of stone to ignore that plea. My brother, who'd become a total squish of a man since he'd married and started a family, wasn't impervious to that plea.

"Hey, let me talk to them," I said.

Liam switched his phone so I could see my nieces. Fiona was a redhead like Mari, while Dahlia had my brother's dark hair, similar to mine. Fiona had always been a daredevil. With Dahlia, she had someone to drag along and use as a baby doll. Dahlia was too sweet-natured to protest, at least for now.

"Hi, Aunt Niamh!" said Fiona. She held up a giant necklace she'd probably pilfered from Mari, too. "Do you like my necklace?"

"It's very pretty."

"Did your mother say you could wear that?" was Liam's question.

Fiona, too smart for a four-year-old, merely batted her lashes and said, "We can put it back before she gets home."

Liam harrumphed. Dahlia waved to me and said something in Two-Year-Old that I couldn't understand but that sounded like, "I peed in the corner," which I was sure Liam was thrilled to hear.

"We're working on potty training," said Liam after he'd hustled the girls back to the living room to watch some TV for a bit. "But Dahlia is stubborn where she isn't loud."

"Mmm, she sounds like me."

Liam laughed. "You were just as stubborn when you were her age. Christ, I was just a dumb kid and had no idea what I was doing, potty-training my little sister. I tried to convince you to just wear diapers for another year, but you'd just take them off and run around arse naked."

I smiled. "Sounds about right."

Liam had pretty much raised me. Our da had run out when Mam had been pregnant with me, and then Mam had passed when I'd been two. Liam, seventeen years older than me, had been thrust into the role of father at way too young of an age. Although I'd grown up with my aunt and uncle, since Liam had felt he wasn't able to take care of me, he'd always been a fatherly figure to me.

Sometimes to the point that he was overprotective. Like right now.

"Back to our conversation," he said brusquely. "How is everything going there? Are you getting enough sleep? Eating right? You're not going to pubs every night, are you?"

"If you're afraid I'm going to get knocked up like Kate, don't worry. I always use condoms."

Liam scowled. Kate was Mari's younger sister, who had a one-night stand in Ireland with Liam's cousin Lochlann. Kate and Lochlann now lived in Dublin with their daughter. Despite a rocky beginning, things had worked out for them.

"Some things a brother doesn't need to know," he said.

"You're the one being nosy."

"Not nosy. Concerned. I don't like you going off on your own like this." His expression turned serious. "After you come home, what happens? What are you going to do with your life? I'm worried about you. It seems like there's not much that holds your interest lately."

I hated how right he was. As a teenager, I'd enjoyed working on cars, but that passion had since faded. Mostly because of the sexism and how I'd been treated too often like a piece of meat around the guys in work-shop. When I'd just wanted to learn how to flush out a transmission, too many of the guys would assume I was too stupid to learn how to do it.

I'd finished college, of course, but the job prospects were scarce. I'd considered staying in New York and living with Rachel and Maddie, but it was way too expensive working a minimum wage job.

So when this whole letter and estate thing had fallen into my lap, I'd jumped at it. It had given me a purpose, something I hadn't realized I'd been seriously lacking.

"I'm only twenty-two," I said, shrugging. "Who knows what they want at this age? You didn't."

"I'm not talking about me. I'm talking about you."

I felt all of ten years old at the moment. My brother had a way of making me feel very young and stupid, even unintentionally. Probably because for my entire life, I'd wanted to make him proud, and at times I'd felt like he'd been too distracted with his own life to notice his annoying little sister.

"I'll figure it out. I always do." My voice was too cheery. "I just graduated from Harvard, and now I'm abroad. I think I'm doing pretty well, all told."

Liam looked unconvinced. "And then what? You'll be thirty, wasting your life at some shite job, alone—"

"What, that's all a guarantee? Come on, don't be stupid. Besides, ending up a spinster with thirty cats wouldn't be that bad." My voice had an edge to it now.

Liam sighed. "I didn't mean it like that. I just want you to be happy and fulfilled."

"Well, yeah. That's the goal, isn't it? But not everyone can be as stupidly happy as you and Mari. Not everybody can have the perfect wife, perfect life, perfect job…" I shrugged. "Sometimes you have to take what you can get."

"My life isn't perfect," he groused. When a crash sounded in the background followed by giggles, he added, "Case in point."

It was right then that I desperately wanted to tell

him about how I was searching for our da. That that was what was important to me right now. But I knew that Liam would try to convince me it was a stupid idea. And if he knew I wasn't even in Ireland but in Paris now with a strange guy, well, he'd probably hop on the next flight and carry me bodily home.

Liam and I were saying our goodbyes when the door to my hotel room opened. To my horror, Olivier came inside—an hour earlier than he'd said he'd be.

"Is someone there?" said Liam, suspicious.

Olivier wandered into the room, but I moved my phone so Liam couldn't see him. "It's just housekeeping. I forgot to put the Do Not Disturb sign on the door."

"Housekeeping?" Olivier sounded offended. "At this hour?"

"Niamh, who is that?" Liam's voice was rising.

"Um, it's no one, I'll talk to you later, bye!" I said the words in a rush and quickly disconnected the call.

I turned to see Olivier, his arms crossed, an amused expression on his face.

"I'm a secret now, am I? How quaint. I have to say, it's the first time someone has wanted to flout that they know a prince," he said.

"Oh my God, shut up. It's not about you. It's about this whole thing." I made a vague gesture.

Olivier cocked his head to the side. "Who was that? Your boyfriend?"

I made a gagging sound. "Okay, *no*. He's my brother. Ew. No. Not my boyfriend." I shuddered.

"Ah." Olivier just watched me put on my shoes. "It'd be immensely awkward, if a lover of yours discovered our agreement."

I stilled. "I don't have any lovers. At least not at the

moment." I tied the laces overly tightly, my foot protesting. I unloosed them and tried again.

"But you don't want to tell your brother about us."

"No, I don't. He's overprotective, and he'll just throw a hissy fit, and who has time for that? No, it's better he doesn't know."

"What happens if you find your father? I'm assuming he's your brother's father as well."

Okay, I hadn't thought about that important point. I'd pushed it away, because there was no guarantee we would find my da. But if we did, well, I'd figure that part out later.

"I'm doing this for me, not Liam. Liam hates our da. He probably wouldn't want to see him, anyway."

Olivier had sat down in a chair and crossed his ankles, like he had nowhere to be. "Your brother cares about you," he said.

"Um. Is that a question?"

His gaze turned faraway, like I wasn't even in the room anymore. "I always wished I'd had a sibling. It's lonely, being the only child. And my parents always had their duties to occupy them."

"My mom is dead. My da might as well have been." I didn't mean the words to sound bitter; it was simply a statement of fact. But Olivier grimaced anyway.

"Yes, I realize this." He rose. "I didn't mean to sound as though I were fishing for sympathy. My apologies."

Well, now I felt like a gigantic asshole. "I didn't mean it like that. Just…" I struggled to explain. "Just that at least you can still talk to your parents, see them, ask them questions. I don't even know if my da really is alive. For most of my entire life, both of my parents have been dead, you know? It was just me and Liam."

"You're lucky." Olivier's voice was soft. "To have someone like your brother, who cares for you so much. I'd give anything…" He trailed off. "Never mind. We need to plan for our trip tomorrow. Let's get dinner and discuss it."

I followed Olivier out of the hotel into a taxi, not caring where we were going. My mind was whirling, though. It was one of the first times I'd seen Olivier vulnerable.

Had he been ignored by his parents as a child? Given off to a nanny while his parents had their own lives? If so, I could imagine it had been a very lonely way to grow up. Although I'd felt abandoned when Liam had asked our aunt and uncle to raise me, I'd always known he'd done it out of love. And he'd been in his early twenties—my age. He hadn't been capable of raising a young child at that age, and I could relate. I could barely keep myself together, let alone think about a kid.

But I'd always known Liam loved me. I'd known Mam had loved me, that Aunt Siobhan and Uncle Henry had, too. Had Olivier ever felt that? Or had his parents' love been frigid, kept at arm's length, while he was raised to be this golden prince who wasn't allowed to be human?

You're more than some arrogant rich boy, aren't you? I thought. I gazed at him as he watched raindrops patter against the taxi window, and I knew that that thought alone was very, very dangerous.

CHAPTER TWELVE

The drive to Jeanne Durand's home took longer than either of us expected. Despite only being a few miles outside of Paris, the traffic crawled at the slowest possible pace. By the time we'd left the city, we were both hungry for lunch and had stupidly not packed anything to eat. I'd almost asked our taxi driver if he had any food, but I hadn't yet gotten that desperate.

When we arrived at our destination, Olivier paid the driver and headed straight for the front door. As for me, I was enjoying taking in the beauty of the French countryside. The address was a little cottage that looked like it had been built centuries ago, although for all I knew it had been built within the twenty-first century. A lovely little garden took us down a path to the front door of the cottage, hanging vines nearly covering the door number.

It was idyllic, straight out of a fairy tale. The bees buzzing, the smell of fresh, blooming flowers, the warm sun. All of it together made me antsy, like an axe murderer was going to jump out of the cottage and run us off of the property. It just seemed way too lovely.

"You look like you're going to vomit," said Olivier blandly after he'd knocked on the front door.

"This place is way too cute."

"And that's why you're looking ill?"

"Yes. I don't trust it." I glanced over my shoulder. I'd tried to peer inside the window nearest the front door, but a curtain had obscured the view.

"I had no idea you were so paranoid." He motioned at me. "Get behind me, then. I'll protect you."

That line made my paranoia disappear, because the image of Olivier protecting my person from some serial killer was hilarious. Olivier could probably hold his own in some fancy-schmancy fencing match, but I really doubted he could take out somebody with an axe.

I was laughing heartily, Olivier glowering at me, when the front door opened. A middle-aged woman with dark hair in a messy bun asked something in French. Olivier asked if she were Jeanne Durand, and the woman, after a moment's hesitation, nodded.

"Do you speak English?" asked Olivier. He gestured at me. "My companion doesn't speak French, I'm afraid."

"A little bit," Jeanne said in a heavy accent. "Are you American?" she asked me.

"Guilty as charged."

At Jeanne's confused expression, Olivier translated into French. She nodded, and after wiping her hands on her apron, she gestured us inside.

"Come, come, have some coffee. We will speak," she said briskly.

Despite the dim light inside Jeanne's cottage, I could make out what could only be dozens of antiques: vases, bowls, statues, clocks. Artwork hung from the walls, while the furniture was heavy and old-fashioned but beautiful. I couldn't help but wonder how much all of this was worth.

Jeanne brought out coffee and some pastries before settling onto a red chair. "How can I help you?" she said.

I looked at Olivier. He looked at me. I finally began. "Olivier says he sold an antique clock to your husband."

At the mention of her husband, Jeanne's expression turned sad. "Many people sold many things to him. But I'm no longer in the business."

"We're merely seeking information. Who did your husband sell it to?" said Olivier.

I brought out the documents that my da had sent to the estate, showing Jeanne the photo of the clock that was enclosed. "Do you recognize it?"

Jeanne peered closely. "*Non*, I do not." She shrugged, returning the papers. "My husband, he sold and bought so many things. He would know, if he were here."

"Is there any possible way we could have you look for any information regarding who he sold the clock to?" Olivier leaned forward. "It's extremely important."

"I can't disclose private information," Jeanne said, rather sadly.

I took a deep breath, my hands shaking a little. "Olivier here is searching for the clock because his mother wants it back. I'm searching for it because we have reason to believe my father has it." I swallowed against the lump in my throat. "I thought for my entire life that my da was dead, but in the last year I've discovered that he's not. Finding this clock will mean reuniting with him."

I gazed into Jeanne's eyes. "If you could have one more day with your husband," I said softly, "wouldn't you do anything to make that happen?"

Olivier stilled next to me. This was a gamble I was taking. Either Jeanne would find it in her heart to help us, or she'd tell us to go to hell and get out of her house.

As the silence lengthened, I worried that Jeanne was considering how she'd throw us out. Or she hadn't understood what I'd said. I was about to ask Olivier to translate when Jeanne rose from her seat and gestured for us to follow her.

Olivier shot me a look. "You're full of surprises today," he leaned down to whisper in my ear.

I didn't have the brain capacity for a clever reply. I was just praying that Jeanne was going to help us, not take us to the back room to be mauled by a rabid bear or something.

"Do you think she understood?" I said quietly to Olivier.

Apparently, my voice wasn't as quiet as I thought, because Jeanne replied, "Yes, I understood."

I blushed scarlet. Olivier chuckled, which made me elbow him in the side. He let out an annoyed "oof," and we were nearly about to start wrestling in this poor woman's hallway when Jeanne led us into a tiny room that functioned as part office, part guest room.

"I don't know if my husband bought or sold this clock of yours," she said, "but I can look in my files."

Olivier replied in rapid French. I could tell by how

quickly he was talking how excited he was. After explaining that he'd sold the clock to her late husband Charles, Jeanne began to look through her files.

It took little time to find the information. It seemed way too easy, just like this cottage was way too pretty.

Stop looking for monsters that aren't there, I admonished myself. *Be happy it was this simple.*

"Here," she said briskly, handing Olivier a single piece of paper.

I stood over Olivier's shoulder. The document was in French, of course, but even I couldn't make out any identifying information. "Wait, is there a name on this thing?" I asked.

Olivier let out a sigh. "It gives the name of an antiques dealer in Berlin." He pointed. "But no name." He looked to Jeanne. "Is this all you have?"

She shrugged. "*Oui,*" was all she said.

When we left Jeanne's cottage after thanking her profusely, we headed back to our hotel. On our respective phones, we began researching the dealer located in Berlin. Despite our best efforts, though, all we could find was a phone number that was disconnected along with an address.

"Of course," said Olivier after we'd returned to our room, the sun beginning to set now. "We can't just call and ask about the clock."

I was brushing out my hair and putting it into a braid. "I think we'll need to go to Berlin."

"That goes without saying." Olivier busily typed into his phone. "I'll book the tickets. Go get us something to eat, will you?"

Annoyance made me reply sharply, "How about I

buy the tickets this round and *you* get us something to eat, oh princely one?"

Olivier raised a single golden brow. "Why so touchy?"

There was no reason for my bad mood. We'd gotten the information we wanted, but perhaps it was that I'd be stuck with Olivier even longer. I gazed at him in the mirror, feeling my heart sink into my toes.

Staying with him any longer was dangerous. But what choice did I have?

"I'll buy the tickets," I repeated.

"I told you I'd finance this trip of ours."

"You have, and I'm grateful. But I want to be able to contribute."

Olivier got up and stood behind me in the mirror. I'd already braided my hair, and he moved the braid over my shoulder. "You never leave your hair loose," he said.

"It's way too long. I need to get it cut."

He pushed a few stray tendrils away from my neck, and I nearly came out of my skin. "Don't cut it. It's too lovely to cut."

Normally I would've told any guy to pound sand with a comment like that, but right then, I wanted to untie my braid and have him play with my hair. As our gazes met in the mirror, heat poured through my veins.

I turned around. "You're way too bossy," I said, but the words were too quiet to sound like a reprimand.

"I'm a prince." He played with the end of my braid. "I'm supposed to be bossy."

I could feel the warmth of his body, standing so closely. He'd unbuttoned his collar, his collarbone visible.

I'd never found collarbones attractive, but here we were.

Some impulse made me stand on my tiptoes. I raised myself up, about to kiss him, when he stepped back. I reared backward, feeling like he'd slapped me.

"Niamh," he said gruffly. "Um—"

I wanted to melt into a humiliated puddle right then and there. "No, don't. I'm an idiot." I grabbed my phone and stuffed my feet into my shoes. "Forget it. A momentary lapse in sanity."

"Niamh—"

I didn't wait to hear his excuses. If I did, I would've started crying, and who wanted to cry in front of a prince?

Nobody, that's who.

～

I WANDERED the streets of Paris, completely unsure where I should go. Mostly I'd just wanted to get away from Olivier.

I decided on going to one of the many bars near our hotel. This one looked like something straight out of the 1920s.

The female bartenders wore flapper dresses with headbands, while the male bartenders had on trousers, white collared shirts, and suspenders with bolero hats. The interior was decorated with all kinds of colorful glass bottles, the lights over the bar in a semi-circle that made it seem almost like a stage.

The bar was full of people, the sound of French moving around me in waves. I wandered to the bar, suddenly wishing I spoke French, mostly so I wouldn't stand out like a sore thumb. After glancing at the menu, I ordered a cocktail called the Green Fairy. Hey, I needed something to make me feel better, okay?

The drink was sweet, fruity, and so delicious that I drank it way too quickly. It was also extremely strong. After just one drink, I felt delightfully buzzed. I ordered another.

As my buzz increased to tipsiness to full-on drunk, the amount of men hitting on me increased as well.

The first one, a Spaniard, had bought me my second drink, his white teeth flashing in the dim light. He was absurdly handsome, his accent was absurdly attractive, and even when he placed his hand on my lower back, I felt a grand total of nothing.

"Do you want to go somewhere else?" he asked me.

I wished I wanted to say yes. Olivier's face, and then the way he'd looked after I'd tried to kiss him, flashed in my mind. At this point, I'd had more than enough alcohol to make very bad decisions.

"Not yet," I finally said, smiling. "I want another drink."

"Of course." The Spaniard—had he told me his name?—waved at the bartender and ordered for me.

Olivier had a right to say no to me. I told myself that, but it didn't make me feel better. It only made the rejection sting all the fiercer. And then a swell of bitterness filled me, because he'd definitely flirted with me since we'd met. He'd touched me—my face, my hair—and he'd looked at like he'd wanted me, too.

I wasn't so naive that I couldn't tell when a man wanted me. Like right now: the Spaniard's wayward hand was coasting up my leg. Goodness, if he kept going, he'd have his hand cupping my crotch.

I considered reacting, but I was way too sloshed to care. Besides, at least one man wanted me.

Even as the Spaniard pressed his advances, a Frenchman joined our little tete-a-tete. He said something deliciously sexy in French, to which I laughed and said I didn't speak French, sorry, but it had sounded nice.

"Is this man, is he bothering you?" Frenchman asked. He had the jawline of a marble statue. It was ridiculous.

I glanced at the Spaniard, who hadn't moved his hand. I shrugged. "I've enjoyed the free drinks."

That made both men laugh. Suddenly, I found myself with men all around me, flirting, buying me more drinks, telling me all about where they were from and asking me about the U.S.

I felt powerful. I felt like the sexiest woman in the entire world.

Until the Spaniard, drunk now, too, cupped my breast and breathed into my ear, "Let's go, yes?"

I pushed his hand away and got down from my stool, only to almost fall to floor. Great, I was *really* drunk. "No boob touching," I said sternly. "I did not authorize that."

"Niamh."

I turned, so quickly that I saw stars. I had to grab onto the edge of the bar to keep from falling on my face.

There was Olivier, his face red, his hands clenched into fists. Great, what had he seen? Had he seen the boob grab? Now I felt gross.

"Oh, it's you," I said. I lurched toward Olivier. "You found me."

Olivier's expression was hard. Harder than I'd ever seen it. "You're drunk."

"How can you tell?" I burst out laughing. I had to grab onto his arm soon after.

"Let's go."

Olivier grabbed my arm. He nearly hauled me from the bar, but not before the Spaniard tried to stop him.

"Who the hell are you? She doesn't want to go with you," said the Spaniard.

Olivier gave the Spaniard a look that you could only call terrifying. It was like the spirit of the haughtiest, richest asshole came upon him and he used all of that power to simply look at the Spaniard like he was a bug beneath his princely shoe.

"We're going," repeated Olivier, his hand still on my arm.

For my part, I was irritated at being treated like some doll. I loosened Olivier's grip on my arm. "I don't want to leave."

"See," said the Spaniard.

Olivier growled. "Stay out of this."

We were attracting attention. The Frenchman who'd also been flirting with me was watching closely, while I could see one of the bartenders tapping something into his phone.

"Shit, come on." I was the one who grabbed Olivier. I wasn't about to get us arrested, especially in a foreign country.

I stumbled through the bar, and Olivier had to help me out the door. I would've been embarrassed, but the nice thing about booze was that you didn't have to feel embarrassed over nearly falling face-first into some strange woman's lap because you could barely stay upright.

"How drunk are you?" Olivier pulled me into the alley in between the bar and another restaurant. The streetlamp overhead illuminated his face. "Do you even care how much danger you put yourself in?"

I burst out laughing. "Danger? Dude, I'm drunk and was having a good time. Nothing happened."

"Nothing happened *yet*. Those men were practically slavering like dogs over you. One of them could've easily gotten you to go with them—"

"And what? We'd had drunken sex? Oh no, call the police. Sounds terrible."

Olivier's face turned red. "You are the most stubborn, idiotic woman—"

I scoffed. "Like you've never gone to a bar, gotten wasted, and flirted with women. Come the fuck on, Olivier. You're just mad because…" I racked my brain. "Honestly, I don't even know why you're mad. You're throwing a fit because, what, I went off on my own? I'm an adult. I can go to a bar and drink my brains out if I want to."

Olivier looked fit to be tied. I'd never seen him this riled. If I'd less alcohol in my veins, I might've tried to figure out why he was so upset. Or maybe the answer would've been a bit more obvious.

But as it was, I wasn't that astute in my inebriated state. I peered up at him. "Why are you so mad?" I wondered aloud.

He pushed his fingers through his hair roughly. "I don't want something to happen to you."

At that, my heart warmed, until he continued with, "I need you to get the clock returned to my family."

I deflated like a balloon. *Pop.* I was only useful to him. Ugh, I hated him. I wanted to go sic all those men who'd been flirting with me to beat him up.

"You know what?" I poked him in the chest. "I don't need this right now. You already humiliated me earlier, and now you're just here to remind me that I'm just a useful tool for you and not that you really give a shit about my safety. And you can go take a long walk into the Seine and drown for all I care. You suck. You're a bad person. I hope you get chlamydia."

To my shock, he yanked me into his arms, his gray eyes dark and stormy. "You're not just a 'useful tool.'" His voice was a growl. His fingers bit into my lower back. "Of course I care about you."

"You think I'm a nuisance and you refuse to kiss me. That's not exactly a five-star review." I didn't care how petulant I sounded.

"You think I'm not attracted to you?" His voice was incredulous. Before I could respond, he tangled one hand in my hair, the other still gripping my waist, and swooped in for a kiss.

I wasn't prepared for that. Even the embrace hadn't prepared me for the heat of his lips moving against mine. I was so shocked that I just stood there, frozen, my brain completely at a loss remembering how to kiss.

But Olivier knew. He coaxed my lips apart, his tongue slipping inside my mouth. I sighed. I reached up and held onto him by the shoulders. I felt dizzy. I felt like I could melt into a puddle right here in the middle of a darkened Paris street.

"Niamh," he gasped, kissing the side of my throat. He said more words in French, the bastard.

But as I was gazing up at the sky, I was just as

suddenly lurching away from him. And then I was vomiting right next to his feet and wishing the earth would swallow me up whole.

Kiss a prince—check
Puke on his shoes—check
Die of embarrassment—check, check, check.

CHAPTER THIRTEEN

The moment the train left the station in Paris, Olivier rose and said, "I'm going to get some coffee," and left me to my own devices.

After my drunken shenanigans last night, Olivier had practically carried me back to the hotel. I'd proceeded to puke a second time—thankfully, in a toilet this round—and had eventually fallen into a restless sleep. It had only been upon awakening that I'd realized that I'd forgotten to book the flight for our trip to Berlin.

When I'd informed Olivier, he had said calmly, "I know. I took care of it."

I'd been simultaneously grateful and annoyed. And I was even more grateful that he'd booked us train tickets instead of a flight, because good lord was I hungover. The thought of being smashed inside a plane for hours was enough to make my stomach lurch.

Besides, according to Olivier, the only available flights would've taken about as long as riding the train. I hadn't had the energy to confirm that tidbit. All I cared about was closing my eyes and trying to work off this hangover.

Oh, and to forget about that whole "kiss and puke on Olivier's shoes" incident.

He hadn't mentioned it. As far as we were both concerned, it hadn't happened. Hell, maybe it really hadn't happened. Maybe it had just been some drunken dream. But considering that I'd seen Olivier cleaning his shoes this morning in the hotel sink, I really couldn't deny that it had happened.

I sighed, pressing my fingers to my throbbing temples. "You're such an idiot," I muttered to myself. "How could you throw yourself at him?"

Okay, to be fair, he'd kissed *me*. He'd been the one to grab me, press his mouth to me, and kiss me like a man desperate for my lips. And because I was just that stupid, my heart did a little flip in my chest at the memory.

Olivier didn't return quickly, and my eyelids were heavy. I dozed off, the motion of the train lulling me to sleep. When I awoke later, it was midday, and Olivier was sitting across from me, sipping coffee and tapping on his phone.

He pointed to a drink next to his own. "I brought you some tea."

My heart flip-flopped again. Even though the tea was already lukewarm and tasted like not much of anything, the gesture was appreciated.

"Thank you," I whispered.

"How are you feeling?"

"Okay. My head isn't hurting as much." I felt my stomach gurgle. "I should probably eat something soon."

"There's a cafe on board. Third car, if you want anything."

"Okay."

Silence fell. I sipped my tea, gazing at Olivier out of the corner of my eye. He had circles under his eyes. Had he not slept, either? Guilt assailed me. I'd been kind of a jerkface to him last night.

"Hey," I said, my voice croaking. I cleared my throat. "Um, last night. I'm sorry about that. I really hadn't planned on drinking that much."

His expression was shuttered. "It's fine." And then he returned to looking at his phone screen, effectively ignoring me.

Fine, I could get that message. He didn't want to talk about the kiss. He wanted to act like it hadn't happened. Although my pride smarted, I knew that it was probably for the best. After we'd found my da and the clock, we'd go our separate ways. I knew that, but it hurt.

Had we become friends in the last week together? I'd certainly gotten to see more of Olivier than just the golden-haired, arrogant prince I'd first met in Dublin. And despite him not wanting to talk about our kiss, I knew that he'd felt the chemistry between us just as much as I had. He could deny it all he wanted, but that didn't make it untrue.

Once again, I wondered if we shouldn't just get each other out of our systems, have some hot, sweaty sex and then move on with our lives.

You think you can do that without getting your heart involved? I asked myself cynically.

Fine, I didn't know. Olivier was different than the other guys I'd had flings with. He was...complex. Frustrating. Beautiful.

Princely.

Sunlight gleamed in his hair as he tapped on his phone, producing a halo-like effect. Even with the dark circles under his eyes and the hint of a beard on his cheeks, he had a dignity about him that made me wonder if it was innate or something instilled into people who were born to roles like he had been.

He glanced up at me. "Yes?"

I looked out the window at the passing countryside. "Nothing."

Olivier returned to his phone, but as I gazed out the window, I could see the reflection of his phone screen in the glass. To my amusement, he was just endlessly scrolling through his calendar. He wasn't adding appointments or opening scheduled appointments. Based on the glazed expression on his face, he was lost in thought.

Right then, his phone rang. I wasn't able to catch the name on his phone before Olivier rose, answered it, and walked away to find some privacy. The irony was that he was speaking in French, so it wasn't like I would've understood the conversation, anyway.

After about ten minutes, Olivier still gone, I got up to find the cafe. My hangover had transformed into being borderline hangry. I made my way to the third car, which was three cars from where we'd taken our seats. The train itself was slick and clearly fairly new. As I walked, I heard smatterings of French, Italian, and German, along with some English.

Outside, the French countryside passed in quick succession. According to Olivier, we'd stop in Frankfurt, Germany, and transfer to another train to finish our journey to Berlin. Along the way to Frankfurt, though, the train would make a handful of stops along its route.

After I'd gotten lunch and probably way too many snacks, I continued exploring the train. It was two floors, with the cafe on the first floor. I meandered down the cars when I heard Olivier's voice. He was tucked into a little nook close to where the two cars were connected. His tone sounded frustrated, and yeah, I'd admit that I stopped and listened for a long moment.

To my surprise, Olivier said in English, "Don't worry about her," before he returned to French. I strained, hoping he'd revert to English again, but despite a few random English words that made no sense without context, I couldn't make anything else out.

I turned to go back up the stairs at the front of the car, but I was so distracted that I didn't see someone walking toward me. I ran smack-dab into a woman, who let out a loud noise of consternation when I accidentally treaded on her foot.

"I'm so sorry!" I said as the poor woman lurched toward an open seat. "Are you okay?"

"Do I seem okay?" she said in a heavy accent. "Did you not see me?"

"No, sorry, um, I can get you some ice—"

The commotion caused a few other people to come around to see what was going on. By the time I'd apologized at least a thousand times, the woman finally telling me she'd be okay, I'd nearly forgotten about Olivier. Until I returned to our seats and he was sitting there, waiting for me, a look on his face that said, "I know you overheard my conversation I'd not wanted you to hear."

Great. Just my fucking luck.

"Want some cookies?" I pulled out the bag, but Olivier didn't take my bribe.

"Were you following me?"

I sat down with a huff. "No. I was getting food and exploring. I just happened to run into you."

"How much did you hear?"

I couldn't make out what he was thinking. His face was blank. He wasn't angry, but he wasn't happy, either. I couldn't help but roll my eyes.

"Even if you'd sat here the entire time, I wouldn't have understood what you were saying, anyway."

He looked triumphant. "So you were eavesdropping."

I bit into one of the cookies that was filled with chocolate and was promptly distracted because it was amazing. I ate another in quick succession.

"So I was eavesdropping on a conversation in a language I can't speak or understand." I shrugged. "I really don't think that counts as 'eavesdropping,' do you?"

Olivier still seemed tense. Because I was a glutton for punishment and was insatiably curious, I couldn't help but ask, "Who were you talking to?"

I really didn't think he'd answer the question. But to my surprise, he said, "My father."

Now, this was getting interesting.

"What other snacks did you buy?" said Olivier suddenly.

I emptied my hoodie pocket where I'd stashed the goods. Olivier snorted when I showed him my bounty. "Did you buy everything available?"

"Pretty much. Hey, I'm hungry. I didn't eat much last night."

Olivier picked out a bag of camembert chips, his expression softening. "I used to eat these all the time as a kid. I haven't had them in years."

"Well, now I'm extra glad I bought them."

Olivier took out a chip, and we ate in companionable silence. But I wasn't about to let the tidbit about his father go to waste. "So what did your father have to say?"

"He wants me to return home."

"Why?"

Olivier shook his head. "He thinks this is a fool's errand."

"You told him what you were doing?"

Olivier hesitated. "In a sense."

"Okay, it sounds like you need to explain that one."

"He knew I wanted to find Mother's clock. He doesn't know, though, that I was the one who sold it all those years ago. Mother didn't want him to know, because he'd be angry with me. So he believes she was the one who sold it."

"Was he angry at your mother for doing that?"

"My mother says he was hurt, but not as hurt as he would be if he discovered I'd sold it to pay off gambling debts I'd accrued. My father loathes gambling." Olivier wiped his hands on a napkin, all class while I was licking my fingers like a total animal. "Apparently, Father had a close friend who became addicted to gambling, to the point that his friend stole from him."

I winced. "Ouch. Yeah, I can see why he'd be pissed at you."

"So he thinks this is just me wasting time instead of taking on more duties as a prince. Even worse, he's pressuring me to marry soon."

My eyes bugged out. "Soon? Like how soon?"

"Within the next year."

I stopped eating at that admission. "But you're not even thirty. What's the rush?"

"He thinks marriage will force me to settle down into the role. A family would tie me down most effectively."

"Well, that's a depressing way to put it. And extremely old-fashioned. Now I'm expecting your father to withhold your inheritance until you father an heir."

Olivier's lips twitched. "You aren't completely wrong."

I scrunched up my nose. "Ugh, gross."

At that, Olivier cocked his head to the side. "Are you objecting to marriage and children in general or the idea of marriage and children with me?"

Shit, I'd walked into that trap. "Neither. Both." I forced my brain to stop freaking out. "I mean, I'm objecting to the idea that you're just some means to an end. That what you want doesn't matter."

"What I want doesn't matter." There was no bitterness to the words. Simply a statement of fact. "When you're born into such great privilege, you're also tasked with the responsibility attached to it. What I want isn't nearly as important as continuing the Valady line."

I felt like I was in some nineteenth-century novel, hearing Olivier speak of heirs and lineage.

"So what happens if you decide to go AWOL?" I asked. "Does your father lock you in the dungeon and throw away the key?"

"That's what marriage is for."

That was a depressing statement. Feeling frustrated

on his behalf, I pressed, "But what if you go off and do what you want? Is that against the law?"

"Of course not, but that would mean disappointing and hurting my family. My father would be devastated." Olivier looked stricken and even angry. "He already expects me to fail. I'm not going to try to fulfill his low expectations of me."

The words were surprisingly bitter. Leaning forward, I said, "I can't imagine he thinks badly of you."

"How would you know?" The words were harsh, making me rear back. "You have no idea what you're talking about."

I scowled at him and crossed my arms. "Geez, sorry I said anything," I said sarcastically. "Return to your scheduled moping and I'll just eat my snacks."

It took a few minutes, but Olivier finally said softly, "Apologies. I shouldn't have taken out my frustration on you."

I was still offended, but I could accept a sincere apology when I heard one. "You're forgiven, but only if you go buy me more of these cookies. That's my demand."

Rising from his seat before bowing, he said, "My lady's wish is my command."

CHAPTER FOURTEEN

My head rested against the warm grass. I groaned, stretching, feeling the rays of the sun on my face. I didn't want to wake up. It smelled so good, and it was so deliciously warm.

Then I heard someone call my name. "Niamh," the voice said. It repeated my name, more forcefully this time. "Niamh."

I opened my eyes. Olivier was lightly shaking me awake, and I realized in a flash that I'd fallen asleep with my head against his shoulder. And to make things even worse, I'd proceeded to drool all over his sleeve.

"We're arriving in Frankfurt," said Olivier. "Wake up."

"I'm awake, I'm awake." I grimaced at the wet spot on his jacket, but he hadn't yet noticed it. I wiped my mouth of any remaining drool. Geez, could I be unsexier?

Olivier pulled at the arm of his jacket. Then he raised an eyebrow at me. "Left me a gift, did you?"

I sank down into my seat. "Sorry. I don't usually drool."

He took off his jacket and stuffed it into his bag. "That jacket cost me over a thousand euro, you know."

I blanched. "Are you serious? Shit, I'll pay for dry cleaning—"

When he began to laugh, I realized he'd been messing with me. "The look on your face…" He kept laughing.

I wished I'd punched him in my sleep. What an asshole. "Why are you the worst person ever? Ugh, why did I agree to this stupid trip to begin with?"

"Because you can't speak French and you needed my money?"

"Okay, nobody needed you to answer."

He just chuckled. When we arrived in Frankfurt, we got off the train and boarded the one to Berlin with saying very little to each other and our trip to Berlin was uneventful. Thank God.

After we arrived at our hotel, it was already too late to go to the antiques store, so we could either stay in or wander around Berlin. I absolutely did not want to hang around our hotel room with Olivier, so I brushed my hair and said I was going out.

Olivier decided to tag along. Part of me almost wished he'd stayed behind, while the other part of me was glad for the company. Our hotel was in the Friedrichstadt neighborhood, near the famous Gendarmenmarkt square that included the Berlin concert hall.

It was a warm summer evening, and all about us were people walking around and enjoying the weather. Olivier and I bought beers at a bar nearby before continuing our wandering.

Soon, the sound of people talking and cars driving along with streets was replaced by the sounds of music. On various corners, parks, and outside buildings were musicians. Crowds of people listened, while others meandered like we were. There were so many people, in fact, that it was difficult to go far without getting stuck in some huge crowd.

"What is this?" I said over the noise of a trombone quartet playing.

"Fete de la Musique." Olivier handed me a flier. "I've attended the one in Paris but never here in Berlin."

"That sounds French, not German."

He smiled. "That's because it was a day invented by a Frenchman. You don't have it in America?"

"Probably, but I've never heard of it being done in Seattle. Then again, I don't pay a whole lot of attention to things like this."

We stopped to grab huge, warm pretzels, and I dipped mine in a spicy mustard sauce as I walked. It was awkward, but even as Olivier laughed at my pretzel-dipping skills, I didn't care. I might be homesick, but nothing could compare to all of the food I'd eaten while abroad.

The moment I'd noted that Olivier hadn't been mobbed by his fangirls here in Berlin, a group of no less than six girls squealed and headed straight for us, practically causing a car crash when they rushed across the street toward him.

"Prince! Prince Olivier!" One of the girls shoved a notebook into Olivier's hands. "Autograph! Please!"

I just kept eating my pretzel. Olivier was cordial, although I could tell he was annoyed at the girls asking for selfies—one for each of them. It got to the point that we began to attract attention.

"Who is that?" said a woman who walked by. "Is he famous?"

I swallowed my bite of pretzel. "Kind of. Have you ever seen that commercial for erectile dysfunction? The one with the monkey?"

The woman made a face. "No. A monkey?"

I kept my expression bland. "Yeah, it's big in the States. Anyway, girls keep mobbing him now. It's kind of annoying, but what can you do?" I popped the last bite of pretzel into my mouth. "I'm so happy he's seeing some success finally."

I leaned over and whispered, "He's convinced this will be his big break. I don't have the heart to tell him otherwise. He sends the commercial to everybody to watch, all the talent scouts. He even sent it to Justin Bieber's agent and thinks he'll be in his next music video." I shook my head. "He has no idea. So sweet, so naive."

The woman nodded, like she really had some idea what I was talking about. "How sad."

Olivier approached us, his gaze darting to the strange woman. He then glanced at me. "Niamh…?"

I looked over at my companion. "Oh, this is who I was talking about. Olivier. He doesn't have a last name. He's like Madonna, or Cher."

The woman reached out to shake Olivier's hand. "Good for you on your success. Don't ever give up, yes?"

"Um, thank you?"

The woman shook his hand a second time, nodded at me, and took off. Olivier gave me a suspicious look. "What in the world did you say to her?"

"Buy me another pretzel and I might just tell you."

"If I'd known the moment I first met you that you were so easily bribed, I would've used that to my advantage."

"The first time we met, you weren't exactly trying to be Prince Charming."

His smile was wry. "I didn't know you'd be important enough for me to charm."

I stuck my tongue out at him, which made him laugh. His laugh felt like golden notes against my skin. It was embarrassing, how easily he could affect me. I thought back to our kiss two nights ago. My cheeks turned red. Olivier's eyes darkened, and for a split second, I could've sworn he was thinking about the exact same thing.

Then the moment ended when a little boy bumped into my leg.

"Let's get you that pretzel," said Olivier.

If I were stupid, I could almost imagine we were on a date as we wandered through the heart of Berlin. Except if I knew very well that if I reached out and took Olivier's hand, he'd look at me like I was crazy.

I glanced up at him out of the corner of my eye. He caught me looking.

So I said, "Why did you kiss me?"

He almost collided into an elderly man. To avoid a full-on human crash, he did a little spin that made him look like he was break dancing. It was hilarious.

Olivier brushed off his clothes, like he'd actually tripped and gotten them dirty. He was still spotless, as usual.

"Based on your reaction, you aren't exactly looking to repeat the kiss." My tone was acidic.

Olivier gave me a strange look. "What makes you think that?"

"Um, two things: when I tried to kiss you, you acted like I had leprosy. Secondly, after kissing me once, you still act like I have leprosy." I shrugged. "I mean, I can put two and two together. You don't think I'm attractive. It's okay."

I was lying about that last part. It wasn't okay. It sucked hardcore. I made me feel like I was about three inches tall and ugly to boot. I knew that as a woman of the twenty-first century I was supposed to not care about male opinions. Sue me, I was shallow.

Olivier stared down at me, his eyes wide. "You think I don't find you attractive?"

"You don't have to repeat it like that."

"I do have to repeat it, because it's the stupidest fucking thing I've heard you say."

We'd stopped in the middle of a square, and people were giving us annoyed looks for blocking foot traffic. But I was only vaguely aware of the crowd.

I could only see the look on Olivier's face.

"Not wanting to kiss you has nothing to do with you," he said finally.

I cocked my head to the side. "Either I'm dumb or that statement was lost in translation."

"Niamh. You are——" He blew out a breath. "You know who I am."

At that, I felt a sting of irritation. "How could I fail to remember that?"

"I mean, nothing that I want to happen with us could ever happen. I'm not meant to marry an American girl. That's not what it means to be the Hereditary Prince of Salasia."

135

I could almost see the crown weighing him down, and for a moment, I felt it, too. It hurt. It really did.

"I think you're insanely attractive," he continued. "And just *insane.* You make me insane, too. You aren't afraid to speak your mind. You live your life without a care what anyone thinks—"

"That's not true."

"You don't care what I think. Do you know how many people I've known who didn't try to flatter me, to cajole me, to get me to do things for them because of my position?" His hands were warm on my elbows. "You, Niamh. You are one of the few people who's ever just seen me as a man, instead of as a prince."

My heart pounded in my throat. I suddenly felt like crying. Feeling completely discombobulated, I was forced back to the present when a passerby's purse knocked into my arm.

"Come on," I said. "Let's get out of here."

We ended up at a park nearby. There were still lots of people, but it was large enough that we could find a little bit of privacy. Sitting on a bench at a nearby garden that overlooked the Spree River, we didn't say anything for a long moment.

Eventually, Olivier took my hand. And my pathetic, lovesick heart nearly imploded inside of me when he raised my hand to his lips and kissed it.

"Don't," I whispered. "Please don't."

He released my hand, albeit reluctantly. His gaze returned to the water below.

I couldn't stand the silence for long. It meant that we were wasting time when we could be talking. Speaking quickly, I said with a breathless laugh, "I had the idea early on to seduce you. To get you out of my system."

Olivier didn't laugh. He just sent me a heated glance. "If you think one time would be enough," he nearly growled, "then by all means, let's return to the hotel."

I'd made a miscalculation. Swallowing hard, I pressed my hands to my red cheeks.

"No, no. I mean, I want to. But it'd probably be a terrible idea," I said.

"Yes, a terrible idea. A very terrible idea."

Except he caught my eyes again, and the look in them made his statement a big, fat lie. I shivered. If we were alone, there was no telling how quickly we'd rip each other's clothes off.

I forced myself to watch a family a few yards away. A child that was probably no more than three years old was currently running away from his mother, and she was chasing after him, red-faced and yelling.

"Wanna bet how far that kid gets before his mom catches him?" I pointed. The boy had run through a flock of geese, causing the birds to honk in dismay.

Olivier narrowed his eyes. The mother was now fending off an angry goose with her hat. "Seems as though he'll get all the way to that tree over there."

"I think he'll get to the bench beyond it. The one that has balloons near it."

Olivier put out his hand, and we sealed our bet.

The little boy ran and ran, which, considering how short his legs were, was pretty impressive. His poor mother had extricated herself from the angry goose and was rushing after her son. The kid was giggling maniacally as he got closer to Olivier's destination, his mother close on his heels.

"Come on, come on," muttered Olivier. When the

boy was able to run past the tree, his mom just narrowly missing picking him up, Olivier swore and threw his hands up. "He can't be running that fast."

"I'm pretty sure he's made solely of sugar and making his mom have a heart attack." We both watched as the chase continued. The boy ran across someone's picnic, the mom stopping to apologize, which allowed him to gain ground again.

But right as he reached the bench, he tripped over something. We were too far away to see. Suddenly, the game was over, the kid was crying, and his mom plucked him from the ground and hugged him closely.

"What do I get for winning?" I said, smiling. "Come on, pay up." Olivier reached into his wallet, but I laughed at him. "I don't want your money."

"Then what do you want?"

I didn't know, but I did know that I wanted to wait to cash in on my winnings. "When I figure it out, I'll ask you for it. How about that?"

"This seems like a terrible idea to agree to."

"Yet you'll do it anyway, won't you?"

Olivier scoffed, but he didn't say no. I smiled, triumphant.

We eventually returned to the hotel, our feet sore from how far we'd walked. Before we reached the building, though, Olivier said quietly, "I meant what I said."

I waited, breathless.

"So I think it'd be best if we had separate rooms," he continued.

I deflated like a sad balloon. It was logical and smart, and it fucking pissed me off that he could be logical in this moment. Stuffing my hands into my pockets, I nodded tightly.

"I'll go talk to the front desk. Here's the key to the room. You can have that one for tonight."

"What if there's no room at the inn?" I quipped.

"Then I'll deal with that, too."

I suddenly had the urge to mess up his hair, to make his cheeks turn red, to see him as upended inside as I was. He moved through the world with so much confidence that sometimes I wondered if he were truly human. I both admired it but, like right now, hated it.

"Then I guess I'll see you in the morning," I said. I was pleased that my voice didn't waver at all.

CHAPTER FIFTEEN

We arrived at the address we'd received from Jeanne early the next morning. After meeting in the lobby, Olivier had been polite but distant. It still snagged at my heart, but I forced myself to put it behind me.

We had more important things to deal with. Like finding this stupid clock and my father. Then again, if he knew the effort I was putting into finding him, he'd probably think it was hilarious. I hadn't known him, of course, but based on what Liam had told me, Connor Gallagher hadn't taken many things seriously. Including his family.

The store was located five miles from our hotel, in the northern part of Berlin. It was a nondescript storefront, except for the creepy mannequins in the window.

One wore a dress straight out of the fifties, a lacy apron tied in the front, while the other mannequin wore a suit that had shoulder pads so large that it looked like a linebacker. Furniture from various eras— leather couches, stuffed velvet chairs, and mod-style tables—were just a few of the items as we stepped inside.

It smelled musty, the lighting garish, but it was filled with people. The walls and the floor were covered with items: vases, furniture, rugs, lamps, dolls, books. I smiled when I found a stack of vintage Harlequin novels on one table. I flipped through one, considering buying it, when Olivier said, "I want to find the owner."

I followed Olivier into the depths of the store. It was a total maze, and I wasn't entirely certain we could find our way back to the entrance.

"Wait, do you speak German?" I said to Olivier. I hadn't even thought to ask him, since I'd gotten so used to him speaking French while we were in Paris.

"Only a little," he admitted.

"What languages do you speak fluently? Besides English and French?"

"Italian, some Spanish. I'd taken German lessons but had never committed myself to learning. A smattering of Russian, as well, but that's a very difficult language to learn if you aren't a native."

I smiled wryly. "Oh, I'm sure." I tried to sound like I knew what I was talking about.

"Do you speak Gaelic?" He weaved his way around a glass table as he spoke.

"Only a little. My older brother speaks it, although he says he's forgotten much of it. I only lived in Ireland until I was six."

"That's a shame. You should try to learn it."

"If I end up staying in Ireland longer term, then I will, definitely. I wanted to get to know my father's side of the family better."

After inquiring about the owner at one of the

handful of checkout areas, we waited for this mysterious person to arrive. Although the employee had said it wouldn't be long, Olivier and I found ourselves waiting for close to twenty minutes.

"Aren't Germans a punctual type of people?" I said. "Unlike the French," I couldn't help but adding.

"Spaniards are much worse at being on time. So are the Italians," replied Olivier. "The French would be in the middle, I believe."

Finally, when the owner came to speak with us, I was about to fall asleep in a very comfortable leather recliner. The owner, a short man with a well-trimmed beard and wearing a Hawaiian shirt and cargo shorts, said in English, "You were wanting to speak with me?"

Olivier rose. "Yes. I apologize that we didn't make an appointment. We weren't able to find a phone number to call ahead."

"Oh, the internet never has it listed right." He put out his hand. "I'm Stefan Bauer. Nice to meet you."

I shook hands with Stefan before he escorted us to his office in the back of the shop. We had to step over a number of items, the hallway packed with even more things. If Stefan weren't the owner of an antiques store, I would've assumed he was just a hoarder.

Stefan's office was more a closet with an ancient computer and even more ancient furniture. I nearly sneezed as dust rose up from the chair I sat on.

"Now," said Stefan briskly, "how can I help you?"

Olivier explained our story, how we'd gotten Stefan's name from Jeanne. Stefan listened, not asking any questions but simply nodding. I interjected where necessary. I didn't want him to think I was some bimbo who couldn't speak for herself.

"So you see, we think you might've sold this clock to my da," I said as I handed Stefan the documents. "His name is Sean Connor Gallagher. I believe it was your store that mailed the documents to my grandda's estate in Dublin."

Stefan stroked his chin. "Ah, yes. I remember this. It was a strange request. The buyer didn't want his purchase to be traced to my store." Stefan wrinkled his nose. "Insulting, like I was dealing with black market goods."

"Oh, I'm sure you aren't," I said quickly.

Stefan leaned back into his chair. "You're correct, young lady. Everything I purchase and sell is always above board. I'll admit, I wasn't entirely sure I'd sell the clock to this person—your father, I presume? It made me suspicious that Durand had sold me a stolen antique. But I'd known Durand for two decades, God rest his soul."

"His widow, Jeanne, provided us with your information," said Olivier.

"Indeed, indeed." Typing on his keyboard now, Stefan said nothing for close to five minutes as he searched his computer. I half-expected him to pull out a floppy disk and hand it to us. I tried to make out his screen, but Olivier kicked my ankle when he saw what I was doing.

Stefan took off his reading glasses. "I can provide you with the address Sean Gallagher gave me."

My heart nearly burst inside my chest. "Oh, that would be so amazing!"

Stefan held up a finger. "On one condition."

I looked at Olivier. Olivier said, "You have a price?"

"Of course I do. We all do." Stefan leaned forward,

and I wondered if he was going to ask us for some absurd amount of money. Or if he needed us to murder his rival, or deliver cocaine to some drug house—

"I want you to come to dinner at my home tonight," he said finally.

Olivier and I said nothing. Eventually, I blurted, "You want to poison us first?"

Stefan blinked then let out a hearty guffaw of a laugh. "Poison you? Good lord, why would I do that? Kill you and then, what, give you the information? My dear, that makes no sense."

Olivier shot me a look that said, *Stop talking, please.* I had to chew on the inside of my cheek to keep from saying something biting.

"Dinner is acceptable," said Olivier finally. "Is that all?"

"Oh no. I'm asking you to dinner because my daughter *loves* royalty." His expression turned wily, his smile wide. "And if I were to bring a prince to dinner, I don't have to buy her the expensive phone she's been begging me for."

"How old is your daughter?" Olivier looked green about the gills.

"Thirteen." Stefan shuffled some papers. "And I'm sure Klara will want to invite some of her friends, too."

Oh God, an entire gaggle of thirteen-year-old girls fawning over Olivier. I nearly choked on my tongue to keep from laughing.

Grimacing, Olivier agreed to the terms, taking a piece of paper with Stefan's address and phone number on it, and then proceeded to glower at me the entire ride back to the hotel as I laughed at him.

~

STEFAN LIVED in a townhouse at the edge of the city. When Olivier and I arrived, the sun was beginning to set, and Stefan ushered us to his rooftop terrace. It was a warm summer night, perfect for eating outside. Before either of us said a word, we were handed beers and shown to a table filled with all kinds of food.

"Wow," I said to Olivier, "who knew the antiques business was so lucrative?"

"That, or he comes from money." Olivier popped an olive into his mouth. "Or his wife does."

Stefan's wife, Luisa, was taller than her husband, willowy where he was squat. Her English was not as strong as Stefan's, and after a few minutes of conversation in English, she floated off to speak with her daughter Klara.

Olivier couldn't avoid the group of young girls who had started giggling the moment he'd stepped onto the terrace. Stefan had brought Klara forward to be introduced, but she was so shy that she'd quickly returned to her friends.

I counted four other girls besides Klara. They all looked about twelve or thirteen. There was one who was especially tall; another was much shorter. The tall girl seemed to find her limbs too long, and she moved with the awkwardness of a girl who was still getting used to her body. The shorter girl kept standing on her tiptoes to get a look at Olivier.

I elbowed him. "So which one will you take as your bridge?"

He nearly spat out his beer. I patted him on the back. "I beg your pardon?"

"One of them would surely accept your suit. Then again, you might just go with Klara. She probably has a huge dowry."

"Please, please, just stop talking."

I gurgled. My gaze caught Klara's, and I motioned for her to come over. She covered her face and then whispered into tall girl's ear. Then the whole group erupted into laughter.

"You're going to have to go over there eventually," I said.

Our gazes went toward Stefan, who raised his drink with a knowing look that said, *Make my daughter happy and you'll get the information you want.*

Olivier groaned. "Why did I agree to this?"

"Dude, they're only young girls. They won't kill you."

He looked so glum that I had to rein in my laughter.

"Have you ever experienced the intensity of teenage girls hanging on your every word? Wanting autographs? Selfies? Asking you intimate questions that you absolutely cannot answer?"

"Can't say I've ever had that problem." I tugged on his shirt. "Come on, Romeo. Let's get this over with."

When we approached, I half-expected the group to turn tail and run. But one of them, a girl with a head of dark, riotous curls, was clearly the leader of the group. She said something in German that sounded like, *Don't be such spineless boobs.* Probably. German wasn't exactly my forte.

"Ladies," said Olivier gravely. He looked like he wanted to throw himself bodily off of the roof.

"What's everyone's names?" I pointed to myself. "I'm Niamh. This is Olivier—"

Group giggle.

"We've met Klara. Who else?"

Curly-haired girl thrust out her hand. "I'm Sofie." Her English was impeccable. She pointed to tall girl. "Astrid." She pointed to short girl. "Mia." Then to the last girl, who hadn't raised her gaze from her feet. "And Anna."

To my immense amusement, Olivier gave them all a flourishing bow. "My ladies," he said, his voice entirely serious. "It's an honor to meet you."

Sofie's eyes lit up. "What's it like to be a prince? Do you get to wear a crown every day?"

"Only on special occasions. They're rather heavy to wear every day."

"You should wear a tiara," said Klara, which made all the girls laugh. "What, he should! He's very pretty!"

"I agree. Olivier would look very pretty in a tiara," I said.

At that, the group of girls' gazes swung toward me. I could sense a mutual feeling of *who is this girl and why is she with Olivier* emanating from them all. I had to admit, I was intimidated. Thirteen-year-old girls could rip you apart with just a few words and a passive-aggressive post on Instagram.

"Are you guys dating?" asked Sofie. She looked at my sneakers, to my ripped jeans, to my worn t-shirt. Damn, I'd felt that in my bones.

Before I could answer, Olivier took my hand and squeezed it. "We are. We met recently but have been traveling together for the past week."

I stared at him. The girls stared at him. Did he want me to get murdered?

"Are we dating?" I gave him an incredulous look then laughed. "That's the first I've heard about it."

No one else laughed. You could've heard a pin drop. No wonder Olivier had been terrified: these girls weren't easy to please.

Astrid was assessing me, her arms crossed over her chest. "Are you American?"

"Guilty as charged."

"How did you even meet?"

Klara shot Astrid a look. "You can't just ask people that," she hissed.

Astrid remained unperturbed. "Why not? Maybe they met on Tinder."

I choked on my drink. This time, Olivier had to pat me on the back.

Sofie's eyes lit up. "How did you meet?" She sighed then put her chin on her hands. "I bet it was super romantic."

"Sofie, do you even know what Tinder is?" This was from Mia.

"Duh, I know what it is!"

The girls began to snipe at each in German. Anna, the shy one, just watched with wide eyes.

"We didn't meet online," said Oliver, loudly. He cleared his throat as five pairs of eyes swung to him. "We met in a library."

I scowled at him. If these girls found out I'd hit him with a book, they might beat me with their phones and upload it on TikTok.

"Oh, like in *Beauty and the Beast*," said Klara.

"Exactly like that." Olivier slid onto the table in front of the girls. "Niamh, you see, is actually very shy—"

I made a face that caused the girls to laugh.

"Don't believe anything she says," continued Olivier. "She's very shy around handsome men, like yours truly."

"I could never talk to a boy like you," whispered Mia.

"Of course you could." Olivier resumed, "Niamh wouldn't meet my eye when we found ourselves in the same aisle in the library. But it must've been fate, because we both reached for the same book at the same time. Our fingers touched…" Olivier let the moment lengthened. "And then the rest is history."

I had to admit, he could spin a tale. I nearly believed that was how we'd met. The girls were now hanging on his every word, rapture in their expressions. Prince Charming had charmed the swarm of adolescents. It was both obnoxious and adorable.

"Now, who wants to take pictures?"

Five hand shot up at once, and then Olivier was in the midst of taking selfies with the girls. I wandered off to the food table. Strangely, I felt a pinch of jealousy. I had no idea why, and it ate at me.

My stomach turned. Suddenly, I wasn't hungry anymore. Turning, I nearly ran into Stefan's wife Luisa.

I apologized, and despite my ruffled nerves, hers seemed completely intact. Despite bumping her arm, she hadn't spilled a drop of her drink. Amazing. I needed to know her secrets.

"Your prince is very charming," Luisa remarked as we both watched the girls ask him questions.

"He can be."

Luisa raised a slim eyebrow. "You sound…envious."

"They're just kids."

"You look at him like my daughter looks at him, you know."

"I do not." I sounded so defensive that I forced myself to laugh. "If you mean I look annoyed, then I would agree."

"You look at him like he's everything you've ever wanted, but he won't pay you the same compliment."

That hurt. I couldn't help but wonder if Luisa had some ulterior motive, but why would she? We would be gone tomorrow. Her daughter had gotten her night with a prince and seemed thrilled.

"I don't say these things to hurt you." Luisa placed a long-fingered hand on my shoulder. "Merely to put you on your guard. I was once an impressionable young woman with a big heart. Like you."

"You don't even know me."

Luisa hummed and sipped her drink. "True. But I've seen that expression on the faces of many of my female friends. Even I was one of them, if you can imagine it."

I felt like I was on a ship that kept rocking back and forth. My legs felt wobbly. My eyes burned, and I hated feeling so vulnerable in front of this stranger.

"I appreciate your concern, but it's not necessary. I'm well aware that Olivier isn't the man for me."

"I hope your heart knows that as well as your mind does, my dear."

I watched Olivier from across the terrace, my heart pounding in my ears. Stefan had joined the group while Luisa sat nearby. When Stefan motioned to me to join them, I put on a strained smile and walked over. I wanted to go hide in the bathroom, but I wouldn't let Luisa see me crack.

If I cracked, it meant that she was right.

Olivier was still telling stories about his life as a prince to the girls. Castles, crowns, horses, the whole nine yards. He told of how he'd dropped one of the royal crowns before his father's coronation ceremony, denting the soft gold. "I'd tried to hide it with paint," said Olivier, "but when my nanny had discovered me, she nearly had a stroke."

Fortunately, the crown had been repaired in time, and Olivier hadn't been tossed in the dungeon. We all laughed, although mine was strained.

Luisa has no idea what she's talking about, I told myself. *You aren't stupid enough to be falling in love with Olivier.*

Yet as I watched him charm all of these people, I felt that prick of jealousy once again. When he caught my gaze and smiled, I wished he'd only smile at me. No one else.

It was selfish, and silly, but I wanted him to look at me and listen to my every word. I wanted him to charm me. Mostly, I wanted that story he'd told about us in the library to be true.

But none of it was true. We weren't dating. We weren't in love. It was all a lie he'd concocted to entertain the girls.

It was all a lie for him.

Yet I had the terrible feeling that it wasn't a lie for me.

CHAPTER SIXTEEN

"You have saved me, Your Highness." Stefan bowed low. "My daughter will never forget this night. So, the information you require in exchange for your service tonight."

As the taxi passed through the city, I gazed at the documents. The documents that included my father's address. Or at the very least, his last known address.

And because my life was absurd, Connor Gallagher just so happened to be living in Dublin, Ireland.

What an asshole. He was right under our noses the entire time.

"You don't seem pleased," said Olivier as we took the elevator to our hotel rooms.

I blinked. "What? Oh. No, I'm pleased. We got what we came for." I folded up the papers, handing them to Olivier, but Olivier pressed them back into my grasp.

"This is your father, Niamh. Not mine. Aren't you excited? Happy?"

At the moment, I only felt tired. Tonight had been

so emotionally draining that I struggled to feel anything about this.

It should feel like a victory. We should be toasting each other and screaming in the streets that we'd gotten this.

Yet why did it feel like a failure? Or, worse, a mistake?

I pasted on a tight smile. "I'm just tired, that's all. Once we return to Ireland, I'll be more excited." At Olivier's skeptical expression, I widened my smile. "See? Happy. So happy."

He said nothing, but based on the look on his face, he remained unconvinced.

I WENT to my room and lay on my bed, staring up at the ceiling. I considered ordering a bottle of wine to drown my sorrows. Instead, I turned on the TV and watched reruns of *The Golden Girls* and ate some German snacks I'd picked up at the train station. Damn, I wish I could be as ruthless as Dorothy or Sophia.

I texted Rachel, mostly because I needed some commiseration. But how did I explain the situation I was in? I hadn't updated her on the whole Prince Thing since I'd spoken to her back when I was in Dublin.

Sending her the longest text ever, I explained as much as I could. The text was so long that my phone had to cut it up into multiple messages. Okay, maybe I should've just called her.

My phone rang. Rachel. Oh shit, I hadn't expected her to call me—

I answered. "Hi?"

"OH MY GOD!"

The conversation proceeded to vacillate between Rachel nearly screeching in my ear, to me attempting to explain, to Rachel going back to yelling at me. She wasn't angry; she just tended to yell when crazy shit went down.

"YOU ASSHOLE. YOU KEPT THIS FROM ME?"

I had to hold my phone away from my ear. "I've been busy," I hedged.

"BUSY, MY BIG TITS! I'M GOING TO STRANGLE YOU WHEN YOU COME TO NEW YORK."

I wasn't scared. Rachel had been threatening to strangle me since we'd first met. It was her way of expressing affection.

After Rachel had calmed down with some help from Maddie, I ended up spilling my veritable guts to them both. I admitted that I was starting to feel things for Olivier and that I hated myself for it.

Both women were silent for a long moment. Then Maddie piped up with, "Are you sure you know how he feels?"

"I mean, he says he's attracted to me. He told me as much yesterday at the park. But beyond that..." I sighed. "Doubtful."

Rachel harrumphed. "I think you're going to have to put on your big girl panties—"

I groaned.

"—and just fucking *ask* him. Because you're both grown-ass adults, and communication is a thing adults need to do."

"We all know you hate the Big Misunderstanding plots," said Maddie.

I could practically see Rachel throwing her hands up. "They just need to sit down and talk! It's so stupid and contrived!"

I didn't want to admit that Rachel was right, because it would mean admitting that I was too much of a coward to ask the question I wanted to ask. And besides, did I really know how I felt? Were my feelings growing, or was I just horny?

"I could be confusing it with lust, you know," I said.

"True," Rachel conceded. "Which is why my next suggestion is that you should really jump his bones."

"I agree," said Maddie. "Get that princely dick."

"Oh my God." I flopped onto the floor. "Did you really just say that to me?"

"Stop acting like a dumb virgin and just get some good fucking. I never took you for a weenie, Niamh," said Rachel.

I sat up, my forehead creasing. "Excuse you, I am not a weenie. I might have ninety-nine problems, but by God, I have a fucking spine!"

Somebody clapped, probably Maddie. "This is so exciting!" she said.

The three of us talked some more, me promising to be brave and talk to Olivier, even though I wasn't entirely certain I could do it. I probably *was* a big weenie.

I had just started watching another episode of *The Golden Girls* when there was a knock on my door. When I opened it, I found Olivier standing there, wearing a robe like he'd been about to go to bed.

"Are you sleeping?" he said.

"I think I'm still awake?" I tried to sound jokey, but Olivier didn't laugh.

"Can I come in?" When I hesitated, he added, "We need to discuss our plans. For returning to Dublin, you know."

Oh, of course. I moved aside, letting him come inside, before putting on my hoodie to cover up my bra-less upper torso. I might have itty bitty titties, but my tank top was so sheer that you could see my nipples through it. And I didn't really need to seem that desperate right now.

"Do we need to fly straight there?" I said, crossing my arms over my chest. "Because I could use a day to just recharge."

"I'd rather not. It would be better to go there straight away, because the address Stefan gave us might not, in fact, be your father's current address. That would add more time to this endeavor of ours."

I sat on the edge of my bed, while Olivier sat in a chair across from me. Although only a few feet separated us, it felt like an ocean. I rubbed my arms, a chill prickling my skin.

"Fine. That makes sense. We can stay at my grand-da's estate."

Olivier began to drum his fingers on the table, and I waited for him to say something else.

"Is that it?" I said finally. "You didn't need to come into my room to ask me this. Should've saved a trip and just texted."

He narrowed his eyes. "Are you annoyed with me? Because you've been prickly all evening."

"Annoyed? No. I told you: I'm just tired." I yawned

widely. "See? Tired. I want to get to bed, actually. If you're going to take care of the tickets like usual——"

Olivier got up and, to my shock, pulled me to my feet. "Why are you lying to me?"

I kept just shaking my head. "I'm not lying. Why are you being so weird right now? It's creeping me out." I plucked his fingers from my arms like they were leeches. "And please unhand me, good sir."

Olivier let me go, but he kept staring down at me. A flush had crept up his cheeks. He looked flustered. It was so weird that I wondered if I'd already fallen asleep and was having a fever dream.

"Was it because I said that nothing could happen between us? Is that you're cold all of a sudden?" he said.

I inhaled sharply. "We both agreed nothing could happen. So I'm not going to be petty enough to take that out on you. Christ, give me a break, Olivier."

"I don't believe you."

I gaped at him. I didn't know what he wanted me to say. In the back of my mind, I heard Rachel and Maddie: *Just tell him.* No Big Misunderstanding, Niamh. Put on your big girl panties.

I took in a shuddering breath. "You want the truth? Fine. I'm starting to have feelings for you, and it scares the living shit out of me, and it's crazy, too, because we've only kissed, so what kind of Hallmark Channel original movie is this bullshit?" With every word, my voice rose. "I barely know you. We're strangers. I think I might just have Stockholm Syndrome——"

Olivier dug his fingers into my hair, and tipping my head back, he kissed me. Hard. I stiffened at first, but soon, I was like melted chocolate in his arms. Liquidy, sticky, and all over him.

I gripped his shoulders, my nails digging into them, as his hands roved down my back. He grabbed my ass and squeezed, while his other hand was busy cupping my cheek. Our tongues tangled as we deepened the kiss. I wiggled against him, and soon I felt his dick harden and press against my pelvis. I wanted to let out a triumphant laugh.

Olivier quickly divested me of my hoodie, and then he was cupping my breasts, watching my expression as he thumbed one nipple, then the other.

"Does this seem like a Hallmark movie to you?" he said gruffly.

I looked down. "Pretty sure boob grabs aren't allowed in those." I sounded breathless and extremely horny.

Olivier pushed one strap of my tank down, then the other, and it was only my arms at my side keeping my breasts covered. I felt a moment of self-consciousness, what with the light still on and my tits being rather fun-sized. But I forced the fear aside. Drawing up my arms, I let my tank slither down to my ankles.

Olivier drank me in. His gray eyes were so dark, they were stormy. His circled his fingers around one breast while cupping the other. "I've wanted to touch these since I first saw you," he admitted. "And when you fell asleep against me on the train, I stared down at them the entire time."

"What a pervert you are." My words turned into a little squeak when he pinched a nipple.

"I kept wondering what your nipples looked like. Were they pointy or puffy? Were they pink or dark red?"

I looked down. "I think they're a mauve color?"

"They look like they should be in my mouth."

Well, I sure as hell wasn't going to say no to that. Wrapping an arm around my waist, he leaned me back before his sucked one nipple into his mouth. It was like my entire body was suddenly aflame. He licked and rolled the nipple with his tongue, and then before I knew it, I was collapsing onto the bed with Olivier on top of me.

He feasted on my breasts until they were tender and red. I could only dig my fingers into his golden hair and hope that I didn't burst into tears from the pleasure. It didn't help that his hands were busy pushing my pants down. Soon, he found the elastic of my underwear and then the soft skin of my pelvis.

"Olivier," I breathed. "What are you—?"

He shushed me. "Tonight is for you."

His fingers found my pussy, and I wasn't even embarrassed at how wet I was already. He delved between the folds, and I could hear how slick I was just from that movement.

Olivier leaned down and whispered French words into my ear. It was so sexy that I could've come right then and there.

"That's cheating. I don't know what you're saying," I complained.

He just grinned. "That's the point, *ma chérie.*"

He then began speaking in Italian, which just beyond annoying. But my annoyance faded quickly, because his fingers were clearly magic, and he knew exactly how to use them. Pushing my panties down along with my pajama pants, I was soon completely naked except for my super sexy cat socks.

He glanced at my socks, which had Grumpy Cat's grumpy visage on them. "Is that a cat?" he said.

"Come on, it's Grumpy Cat. Do you even internet? May she rest in peace."

He shook his head, laughing softly. Then my stupid socks were forgotten the moment he pushed my legs open and parted my pussy folds. He slicked one finger through them. "You're soaking wet."

I didn't have a response to that. And I especially had no response when he pushed one finger, then another, inside me. My pussy contracted around them. When he leaned forward and began to click the straining tip of my clit, I had to bite on my lip to keep from crying out.

He teased my clit with that devilish tongue. When he upped the pressure, I let out a little squeal.

"Too much?" he said.

I nodded. "It's really sensitive."

I'd had sex with guys who'd thought that mashing the clit with their thumb as hard as possible was the way to a woman's heart. Maybe for some women—no shame —but definitely not for me. I preferred a lighter touch.

Olivier licked around my clit, and it was just enough yet not enough pressure that I squirmed. He pressed his fingers upward in that dangerous come-hither gesture that, combined with clit action, was the perfect recipe to send me straight into orgasmic bliss.

Soon the only sounds in the room were his fingers moving faster, the sound of my pussy nearly gushing as he played with me. He groaned when I bucked against his lips.

I could feel my orgasm starting in my toes. My eyes nearly rolled back in my head. "Olivier," I gasped.

He didn't let up. He licked a little faster and rubbed

a little harder inside. My orgasm slammed into me so hard that it was a good thing I was lying down. I screeched like some crazed banshee. I bucked so hard that I nearly hit Olivier in the chin with my crotch.

Olivier just laughed and drew out my orgasm. I kept shuddering and shaking, my fingers digging into the comforter, my toes curling. When he was able to make me come a second time, I wanted to commission a statue in his honor.

"Oh my God," I kept saying, aftershocks sparking through me. "Oh my God."

Olivier crawled up the bed to lie beside me. He kissed me, his fingers still wet with my juices. It was so hot that I moaned into his mouth.

I reached down to rub his dick through his pants, but he gently pushed my hand aside. "Tonight was just for you."

I was so drowsy from my double orgasms that I didn't have the heart to protest. I yawned widely, blushing at how loud it was.

Olivier smoothed my hair from my forehead. "How are you feeling?"

I didn't have the words to describe how I was feeling. It wasn't just the physical pleasure. My heart was practically in my throat. I gazed up at him, dangerous words on my tongue. But I swallowed them.

Because at least we had this—this temporary, incendiary thing.

"I'm good," I said hoarsely.

Olivier pulled me close, wrapping his arms around me. I buried my face in his chest. He stroked my back, whispering words in French, until my eyelids got heavy and I fell fast asleep.

CHAPTER SEVENTEEN

I woke to the sound of rain. Yawning, I stretched my arm across the bed, only to find myself alone. Olivier must've returned to his room. Disappointment slashed through me, until a minute later the door unlocked and he came bearing coffee and pastries.

I might be able to resist an actual prince, but I couldn't resist a handsome man bearing food. He smiled at me as he handed me a latte.

"I bought a few different pastries," he said, "since I wasn't sure which one you'd like."

My eyes lit up as I looked at the array of food. I ended up choosing one that looked like a coffee cake but was denser and had sliced almonds scattered across the top. Olivier chose one that had strawberries and strudel as its topping.

After we finished eating, Olivier said, "How are you feeling?"

I almost blushed like a schoolgirl. The night before came roaring back, and I could almost feel the sensations he'd awakened in me again.

"Um, fine. You?"

He licked his thumb. "I woke up with a major case of blue balls. I had to go to my room and, ah, take care of it."

"You could've woken me up, you know. I know a few good ways to cure that particular illness."

He smiled. "It's fine." He wiped a crumb from my bottom lip, and I touched his thumb with my tongue. He inhaled.

"Why don't you want to have sex with me?" At the moment, I was mostly just curious. Most guys wouldn't have hesitated. Hell, most women wouldn't have hesitated. I'd jump his bones right then and there if he wanted some good dicking.

"I want you. Don't believe otherwise." His eyes darkened, his thumb continuing to trace my lips. "I want to see these pretty lips wrapped around my cock. I want to fuck you until you scream my name, your pussy squeezing me like a vice."

Well, okay then. If he didn't want to turn me on again, he was doing a terrible job of it.

"Now I'm extra confused," I said.

He drew his hand away. "If we were to date, it would change your life irrevocably. Although I can move about fairly freely here and in other countries, in Salasia, I'm never alone. The paparazzi follow me wherever I go, and they follow anyone associated with me. Especially any woman I'm dating."

"I'm not scared of getting my picture taken."

"It's not the photos—which are invasive, and they're always wanting to get a controversial shot. The split second you step out of a car and accidentally flash your panties? They'll sell that image for millions, and it'll be on the internet forever. The moment your skirt flies up? When you're sunbathing topless somewhere private, but they camp out kilometers away with a long-lens camera and still manage to take photos?"

I held up at my hands. "Okay, okay. I get it."

Olivier sighed. "And then what's written about you in the papers." His expression turned dark. "It's vicious. Absolutely vicious. When I dated Aimée, she accidentally spilled some wine on her gown during some event.

"I don't even remember what it was for. The press spun the whole thing into making it seem as though she was a drunkard. They ended up nicknaming her Alcoholic Aimée, although that's the English translation."

"Holy shit."

"I couldn't even blame her for cheating on me. She was miserable. Although I wasn't the one who wrote those things, it was being with me that caused it."

"That still doesn't give anyone the right to cheat. She could've just ended things instead of sneaking behind your back." I wasn't much for dissing somebody's ex, but I had to admit, if Aimée were in front of me right then, I wouldn't have offered her one of our pastries.

"Perhaps." Olivier shrugged.

"You sound way too calm about the whole thing. Any guy who cheated on me would have a death wish. If not from me, from my brother." I shuddered at the thought of Liam finding out I'd been cheated on. He'd go on a murderous rampage.

Olivier raised an eyebrow. "Yet you haven't told your brother about us?"

"What's there to tell?" I shot back.

"Now you're being defensive."

I growled, crossing my arms over my chest. "He just gets way too overprotective. He still treats me like I'm a little kid. I'm not six years old anymore, but it's like he still sees me like that. It's frustrating."

"He cares about you."

"Of course he does. That doesn't mean he can try to control my life, either." I gave Olivier a pointed look. "You can't tell me you enjoy your parents controlling your life."

"They don't control my life," he said dryly. "It's more our way of life that does."

"Have you ever had a say? In where you went to school, what you wore, what you said to the press?"

"As a child, no. As an adult, to some degree. But it's important to present a united front to the public. One member of the royal family going rogue hurts everyone. It tarnishes the reputation we must uphold. As sovereigns, we don't get to make choices like private individuals. It goes hand in hand with the job description."

"What are your parents like? I don't think you ever told me. You already know about my brother, who's basically been a father to me." I then told Olivier about being raised by my aunt Siobhan and uncle Henry, including the day that Liam left me with them. It had only been when I'd been much older that I'd understood why he'd done that. As a child, it had seemed like he'd not wanted me anymore.

"Do you remember your mother?" said Olivier.

I shook my head. "I was only two when she died. Liam has told me stories about her, though." I pulled out my phone to show Olivier a photo of me, my mom, and Liam. It was taken a few months before Mam died, and despite her smile, you could see the dark circles under her eyes along with the scarf around her head that showed how sick she was.

"She's beautiful," said Olivier. He then said, "And you look exactly the same."

"Minus the baby mullet, you mean." My hair had grown in slowly after I'd been born. As a toddler, it had eventually grown into a cute little mullet that had stuck around until I was almost four.

"Liam always told me how happy Mam was when she discovered she was pregnant with me. She'd had cancer and had gone into remission, but her physicians had told her that most likely she wouldn't be able to conceive again. She said that I was her miracle baby." I smiled. "When I was born, she decided to name me Niamh because it means 'radiant.' I was her radiant one."

I felt my throat clog with tears. Even though I hadn't known her, I missed her. What would she say about Olivier and this adventure we were on? Would she have wanted me to find Da? She'd loved him, even after he'd abandoned his family, at least according to Liam.

Olivier took my hand, not saying anything. But I could feel that he cared through that simple touch. It was strange, I thought, how I was now able to be vulnerable with him when not too long ago, I would've rather swallowed my tongue than say these things in his presence.

"What about your parents?" I wrapped my arms around my knees.

Olivier's gaze turned far away. "My parents were a love match, or at least my father has always claimed it was. My father says that the day he met my mother, he fell in love.

"He called her and left a voicemail to go on a date with him, neglecting to mention he was the next in line to the throne. It took three more phone calls before she agreed to a date. It was a month later that they were engaged."

"Goodness, your father moves fast."

"I don't know if my mother reciprocated his feelings. She was much younger than him, only nineteen when they married." He looked at me. "Not much younger than you, I think."

"Is your mom Salasian?"

"Yes, from the lesser aristocracy. She's the grand-daughter of a marquis. My grandfather, Prince Louis, didn't approve of the match, however. My mother brought little money or influence with her, and there'd been some kind of scandal surrounding the family a few years before she met my father. But they married anyway."

"Sounds romantic. Like out of a fairy tale."

"If it started out as a fairy tale, it didn't last long. My parents stopped sharing a bed by the time I was five years old. The only reason they never divorced is because it would be a stain on the royal family. My mother is also deeply religious." Olivier's lips twisted. "Only a dispensation by the Pope himself would compel her to divorce. Even then, I don't think it'd be enough."

Olivier then told me that his parents had never fought. It was more that they'd transformed into platonic friends who happened to share a son and were married. They weren't physically affectionate with one another, as far as Olivier had ever seen. They lived separate lives, had separate friends and hobbies. They only spent time as a couple and as a family when in the public eye.

He told me about how he'd preferred sports and hunting over books and learning about politics like his father, Prince Etienne. When Olivier should've been attentive in class, he was getting in trouble for passing notes to friends and pulling on girls' pigtails. He was rowdy where he should've been a paragon of good behavior, even as a child.

"So I leaned into being the bad child, because no matter how hard I tried, it was never good enough for my father." Olivier shrugged. "I've done little to change his beliefs in that regard since then."

I wanted to reassure Olivier, that surely his father loved him and didn't think of like that. But what did I know? Perhaps Prince Etienne truly did see his son as a feckless and immature failure. Perhaps he'd wished he'd had another son that had been more in his image.

I realized that we'd both been parentless, just in different ways. It made me want to hug him. I wanted to tell him I didn't see him as a disappointment, this prince I barely knew yet felt as though I'd known him for ages.

"So you see," said Olivier, his tone turning wry, "anyone who dares to date me is probably a little bit insane."

It was difficult to wrap my head around that kind of life, the life of a royal. And as I tried to grasp it, I realized that anyone who dated Olivier would be expected to behave like a royal, regardless of lineage. The mere thought of it made me feel ill.

Sure, there were jewels, estates, and the opportunity to travel the world. You were treated like you were genuinely special and important simply by the virtue of your birth. There was some appeal to that, I supposed.

But all of the money in the world couldn't make living in a gilded cage appealing. And I knew without a shadow of a doubt that if this thing between us continued, I would be miserable sharing that cage with Olivier.

"This sucks," I said.

He didn't need me to elaborate. I hadn't meant to ask this question. But even as I told myself it was a stupid idea, I said the words anyway. "If you were just a regular person...?"

Olivier just smiled sadly. "Yes. The answer is yes." Taking my hand, he stroked my palm. "No matter what happens," he said quietly, "I'm glad we met."

Stupidly, I felt tears prick my eyes. I sniffled and squeezed his hand. "Yes. Even if you're extremely annoying most of the time."

He didn't laugh. He just leaned forward and kissed me, his lips feather soft, before returning to his room.

CHAPTER EIGHTEEN

Two days later, we were back in Dublin. Rain poured from the sky as we traveled to my da's last known address. Located on the west side of Dublin, it took about a half hour to get there from my grandda's estate.

No, *my* estate. It was mine in all but name. Once I found my father and Mr. McDonnell had the proof he needed—what that would entail, I had no idea—it would be mine.

When I'd been little, Liam had told me a few stories about our dear ole da. He'd been reluctant to share them, as if by talking about Connor Gallagher, it would somehow make his abandonment of us acceptable. I'd cajoled and begged Liam to tell me anything. I'd heard stories of Mam, but not Da. If he was included in a story, it was only in passing.

"He was a drunk and he left," Liam had said gruffly. At the time, he'd been visiting me in Olympia, where I lived with my aunt and uncle. I'd started second grade the month before, and I'd been waiting for Liam to visit for weeks.

"Mam must've liked him," I pointed out.

Liam grunted. "Mam had a soft heart." He ruffled my hair. "Just like you."

I wrinkled my nose and stuck my tongue out at him, belying his words. "Come on, just one. I won't ask again for another." I crossed my heart. "Cross my heart, hope to die, stick a needle in my eye."

"Bloodthirsty little wench. Fine. Here's a story." Liam cleared his throat, like he was about to put on a performance.

I watched him in rapt anticipation.

"Long before you were ever a twinkle in Mam's eye, Da woke up one morning and decided to drive us all the way to the Cliffs of Moher. I was maybe seven or eight. I'd never seen it, and Da just decided he wanted me to. Mam, bless her soul, didn't have the energy to remind him that it was over two hundred kilometers away."

Liam looked over at me. "Do you know what the Cliffs of Moher are?"

I shook my head.

"Well, whenever we go back to Ireland, I'll take you to them. They're these huge cliffs overlooking the Atlantic Ocean, and there's a legend that a woman chased after a man who didn't return her feelings. He was nimbler than her on those cliffs, and she tumbled to her death. It's called Nag's Head because of that."

I scowled. "Nag's Head? That's not fair. She was just trying to tell him how she felt."

"Maybe. Or perhaps she should've just left him well enough alone." Liam pointed at me. "A good reminder to never chase after a man if he doesn't return your affections. A man should be chasing after you."

I filed away that tidbit of advice for later. Liam went on to tell me how Da hadn't packed anything to eat on the way there, and they got a flat tire halfway there. Da was swearing and stomping as he replaced the flat with the spare, Mam trying to keep him calm. Liam had been complaining that he was starving, and Da had told him to stop whining, they'd eat soon.

By the time they arrived at the Cliffs, it was nearly dark. Da hadn't taken into account the time of year. Mam, being the sensible one, hadn't chastised him for it. She'd merely advised Liam not to go too far. She didn't want him plunging to his death.

"Da scoffed at Mam being so overprotective. He let me go to the very edge of Nag's Head, and I'll always remember looking down at the crashing waves, the sunset streaking the horizon. I felt like I was at the edge of the world."

Liam's mouth twisted. "Then I nearly fell straight off the edge when I turned around and stepped on a rock. Da caught me by my shirt, Mam screaming herself silly. I started crying, but after making sure I wasn't hurt, Da told me to buck up and that I was fine."

The story ended there. I didn't know how to respond. It wasn't the happiest of tales, and it didn't make me wish I'd known my father. He sounded like he wasn't very nice.

"That day taught me that although Da would take me to see something like the Cliffs of Moher, he didn't much care how I felt about it." Liam gave me a sad look. "So you see, that's one reason why I'm not so sad that he took off."

I didn't know what made me think of that story that morning, as Olivier and I traveled to my da's address. Then again, perhaps my subconscious was warning me, reminding me not to get my hopes up.

Had I dreamed of my da showing up one day and telling me he loved me? Of course, when I'd been too little to understand why he'd left. Even as I'd gotten older and Liam had told me more about him, I'd still let myself dream about such things. The reality and my hopes were at odds for many years.

And if I were honest with myself right now, there was still a small part of me, that little girl full of dreams, who hoped that her father had changed and would say all the things I needed to hear from him.

It was still pouring rain when we arrived at our destination. My heart was hammering in my chest as I gazed up at the old house, the taxi having already driven off. We didn't know how long we would be.

I'd brought an umbrella, and the rain pattered softly on its surface. Olivier took my hand, my fingers cold, and squeezed it.

"Ready?" he said.

"No," was my honest answer.

"We can come back later."

I huffed out a laugh, my breath steaming in front of me. "Then I'll never get the courage to do this. No, let's even see if he lives here."

At the front door was a callbox. We hadn't been given an apartment number from Stefan, so we had to page through the names. When we reached the G's, I was gripping my umbrella so hard my knuckles were white.

Gallagher, Connor. There it was. Apartment 405.

"What if he doesn't let us in? What should we even say? Should we lie and say we're selling something?" My words were stumbling off of my tongue.

"I think you should say exactly who you are: Niamh Gallagher, his daughter."

I swallowed, hard. I input the extension, and it rang. And rang. I was about to give up when a voice answered gruffly, "Yeah?"

I couldn't breathe. Suddenly, my voice dried up in my throat. I had to take two deep breaths before I squeaked out, "Um, it's me. I mean, is this Connor Gallagher?"

"Who's asking?"

Olivier gave me an encouraging look, nodding.

"It's Niamh. Your daughter."

Silence. A car splashed water onto the sidewalk near us, and I could hear some poor pedestrians yelling at getting soaked.

My ears were ringing. I barely felt Olivier put an arm around my waist when I heard my da say, "Come on up."

The front door buzzed. Olivier pushed it open. Inside was a small, cramped lobby that contained two faded chairs and mailboxes on one wall. There was no elevator. We began the climb upstairs, the staircase squealing with every step. Lights flickered overhead. It smelled musty, the walls damp from the humidity.

When we reached the fourth floor, I stopped, but Olivier beckoned at me to continue. "This is the third story."

I looked at the door numbers. He was right. Shit, I'd forgotten that Europeans did stories differently than we did in the States. I hadn't paid much attention in Paris and in Berlin since we'd always taken the elevator.

"That's just absurdly confusing," I grumbled, trying not to start panting as we finally reached the correct floor. "How can the first floor be floor zero?"

"It's the ground floor."

"Which is the first floor."

"You Americans. Always have to do things differently when the rest of the world uses the metric system and ground floors."

I was smiled, but it was kind of wobbly. The stair climb had calmed my nerves a little. I wiped the sweat that had beaded on my upper lip.

"Is my face super red?" I said, suddenly feeling self-conscious.

Olivier's expression was almost sad. "Your face is perfect."

I knocked on 405, and then before I could think too hard about running in the other direction, the door opened. And then I came face-to-face with the man who'd given me half of my DNA but who'd never even met me.

We assessed each other in silence. The photos I'd seen of Connor Gallagher had been over twenty years old, and the lines on his face and his receding hairline showed his age. Despite that, he looked so much like Liam that I struggled to find words.

"So it really is you," said Da finally. He held the door open. "Come in, then."

Da's apartment was tiny with little in the way of furniture. There was an old futon that must've also served as his bed on one wall, a TV on the other.

Various wrappers and cigarette butts were scattered across a nicked coffee table. There was a whistle from the kitchen that signaled a kettle boiling. It smelled like sweat and tobacco.

Da brought two rickety chairs from the kitchen table for me and Olivier to sit on. He brushed dust off the leather and gestured. "Sit. I'll get tea." He then sliced his gaze to Olivier. "And you are?"

Olivier put out his hand. "Olivier Valady. I'm Niamh's…" He hesitated. "Companion."

My da grunted and, after shaking Olivier's hand, disappeared into the kitchen. When he returned with tea, he gave us both steaming mugs before sitting on the futon across from us. He pulled out a cigarette and said, "You mind?"

"It's fine," I said. At least the one window I could see was open.

Da smoked and looked at me. I kept bouncing my foot against the floor, feeling my armpits get sweaty again after our staircase climb. I hoped I'd put on enough deodorant today.

"So, you found me," Da said after blowing out a puff of smoke. "How'd you manage that?"

"Olivier helped me. That's why we're here together."

Silence. Then I forced myself to ask, "How are you? It's nice to finally meet you."

He shrugged. "Been better. Sorry about the state of this place. If I'd known I'd have company, I'd at least have taken out the rubbish." He laughed, the sound turning into a deep cough soon after.

He drank his tea in quick gulps. "Fucking bloody

hell," he muttered. "Oh, don't worry about me. I've had this cough as long as I can remember."

I couldn't help but notice that Da looked very thin. His skin was pale, and there were dark circles under his eyes. As he lifted a cigarette, I could see his hands shaking a little. Although he wasn't much older than sixty, he looked at least ten years older than that.

As I struggled to know what to say, Olivier interjected into the silence. "I've actually accompanied your daughter for a specific reason. You see, I'm in search of a particular antique." He pulled out the documents he'd carried across the Channel and back again. "This clock. We were given information that you possessed it."

Da took the papers without his expression changing. He pulled on his cigarette before finally putting it out against the coffee table. "Why do you want to know?" he said.

"That clock was—is—my mother's. You see, I sold it a few years ago for a very selfish reason, and I've been searching for it ever since. It would mean everything to my mother if I were to return it to her."

Da narrowed his eyes at Olivier. "You're not from around here, are you?" He leaned back into the futon. "Where are you from, anyway?"

"He's French," I said. I didn't look at Olivier, but I really didn't want Da to know about the whole prince thing. "We were just in Paris, actually, searching for you."

Da had no response to that. He eventually rose from the futon and went around the corner to the kitchen. A moment later, he returned with the clock we'd been searching for in his hands.

"Oh my God," I said, because it was hard to believe the thing existed. But when Da placed it on the coffee table in front of us, we all knew it was exactly the antique Olivier had been searching for. The hands of the clock ticked the time, which was two hours off from the current time.

"So you went to all this trouble to find me for a clock," said Da. "It must be very important to your mother."

There was an edge to those words that I didn't understand. Olivier caught them, too, his brow furrowing. "It is, yes. And I'll pay you any sum if you'll sell it to me."

"Any sum? My boy, that's no way to barter. Now I'll fleece you silly and you'll go home with a smile on your face."

"The sum is inconsequential."

Da's gaze turned to me. "So this one has told me why he's here. Are you here for the clock, too, daughter o' mine?"

My stupid heart squeezed inside my chest. I'd warned myself not to get my hopes up. But sometimes the heart was a stupid organ, and it could cling to hopes like that poor woman who'd fallen off the Cliffs and gotten called a nag for her trouble.

"I'm here because I wasn't sure you'd even speak to Olivier without me. Clearly, I was wrong."

Da let out a gruff laugh. "Who said you were wrong? No, no. I'm glad you came." His green-eyed gaze took in my face, and for one split instant, I could see his expression soften. "You look just like your mam. A spittin' image of her."

But the tender moment ended as soon as it had

occurred. All business, Da said to Olivier, "I'll consider your generous offer, but I'll make no decision this evening."

He turned back to me. "Come back tomorrow to see me—alone. Then I'll make my decision."

CHAPTER NINETEEN

I was frazzled when I arrived the following day at Da's. I'd woken late, my phone not going off for some reason. Olivier had gone for a walk, so he hadn't been there to wake me. I'd hurried through my shower and had almost forgotten my wallet. I had to run back inside the estate, nearly mowing over poor Cara in the process.

Now sitting once again in Da's apartment, I waited for him to make me a tepid cup of tea for a second day in a row. The clock still sat on the coffee table. I had the urge to wipe down the surface of the table. Surely the clock was too valuable to sit on a bunch of cigarette ash and wrappers.

Da handed me my cup of tea that tasted like dishwater. After lighting a cigarette, he said, "Do you know who your companion is?"

The question startled me so much that the tea sloshed in its mug. Luckily it wasn't too hot, but I had to dab at my jeans with a stray fast-food napkin as my mind whirled.

I decided that honesty was my best bet here. "Yes, I know who he is. How do you?"

Da's lips lifted in a wan smile. "You know he's the Hereditary Prince of Salasia, then? The only son of Prince Etienne?"

"Yes. He told me so himself not soon after we started traveling."

Da smoked in thoughtful silence. He seemed calmer today. "How's Liam?" he said suddenly.

"Liam? He's doing well." I said the words with an edge, knowing that Da hadn't even bothered to ask about my brother yesterday—or in the twenty-two years he'd been on his own. "He's married, you know. He has two girls, and he's a professional photographer. He lives in Seattle."

Da let out a puff of smoke. "Good for him," was all he said.

"Yes, good for him. He's very dedicated to his family. He'd do anything for them, and he's sacrificed a lot to raise me."

Sighing, Da stubbed out his cigarette and regarded me. "You're mad. Understandable. I'd give you an explanation, but what would it matter? What's done is done."

"Most people would give an apology."

"Is that what you want? You want me to say sorry, give you a hug, and tell you everything's good? Lass, I know you don't want that. You're obviously smarter than that."

I had half of a mind to storm out of his apartment. Or at the very least to throw one of his ashtrays at his head. But I didn't want him to see how much his words hurt me.

He might be my father biologically, but beyond that, he was only a stranger. Liam, and then my uncle Henry, had been my fathers in Connor's stead.

"You said you know about your handsome prince. Did he mention to you that he'd come to see me this morning? Based on your face, I'm going to venture to guess that that is a no."

"Why would he come to see you without me?"

"Because I asked him to."

I felt like a broken record. "Why? To discuss the clock?"

Da let out a rough laugh. "The bloody clock. No, it's not about the clock. Not precisely." His smile was wry now. "You have no idea what I'm talking about, do you?"

"No," I said, irritation lacing my voice.

He reached over, pulling a metal pin from the shelf below the coffee table. He fiddled with something on the back, his tongue touching his teeth. Then a moment later, a little drawer popped open near the bottom of the clock.

He handed it to me. Inside the tiny drawer were papers. I touched the edge of one.

"Read what's on them," said Da.

I gently extracted the papers. Unfolding them, I discovered that they were letters. My heart pounded in my chest, and I was glad I was sitting down, because I felt a little dizzy. Licking my dry lips, I began to read the first letter.

It was addressed to someone with the initial A, dated over twenty-five years ago.

My darling, I know we can overcome anything. We're meant to be together. I love you with all of my heart.

The letter was signed by C.

I looked up at Da, but he just gestured for me to keep reading.

I unfolded another letter, and my eyebrows rose to my forehead. This letter was more explicit. *I want to lick your lovely tits, suck on your toes. I want your cunt dripping into my mouth. Meet me in rose tower on the south lawn tonight.*

I blushed to the roots of my hair, mostly because Da was watching me read this. Geez, talk about awkward.

The letter also included a line that stood out to me: *Do you think you should keep the baby?*

The last letter was essentially a farewell. C wrote that he was moving to Belgium and that he wanted to end things. Although he'd enjoyed his time with A, these things couldn't last forever. She understood, yes? This time, though, the writer had addressed the receiver not as A, but as Alex.

"Okay, what are these all about?" I said after I'd folded them up and had returned them to the drawer. "You wanted me to come over here to read some dirty letters from some randoms?"

Da smiled. "Not from some randoms. Those letters were written to Prince Olivier's mother, Princess Alexandra. And not from her husband."

"What?"

"Don't you understand already? Your golden prince is a bastard. Look at the dates. A year before Alexandra married Prince Olivier's father."

If it started out as a fairy tale, it didn't last long. My parents stopped sharing a bed by the time I was five years old.

"You don't know that for sure."

"I didn't, until I spoke with Olivier this morning. He doesn't have much of a poker face, you know. It didn't take much for him to confirm those letters were addressed to his mother and that the dates would line up with his own conception." Da waved a hand. "Oh, he didn't say as much. But he said enough for it all to line up."

I couldn't breathe. Olivier was a bastard? But these letters, if they were written to his mother, were damning. Had she been pregnant when she'd met Prince Etienne? Had he known?

"What do you want?" I said to Da. "Money? Because Olivier already told you he'd pay any price for the clock."

Da sighed, like I was too stupid to understand everything. "Why do you think I wanted this clock in the first place?"

"How about you tell me, since you're the one with all of the answers," I shot back.

"I knew you'd be a handful."

"You weren't even there when I was born. You ran off, remember? Did you even know that Mam had had a girl?"

"I got her letters, if that's what you're asking."

The admission hurt. I could almost, *almost*, forgive him if he'd somehow fallen out of contact with my mom and had had no idea I'd existed. Well, except he'd known about the pregnancy. No matter how I tried to justify his actions, there was nothing that could make them acceptable.

I suddenly wished I'd never come here to find him. The only silver lining in all of this was that I'd met Olivier.

"I wanted the clock," said Da, interrupting my silence, "because it was my mother's, years ago. Your grandmother Mary, who died when I was..." Da screwed up his mouth, thinking. "Ten years old. Just a stupid kid. She died in a car accident, and your grandda never really got over it."

I thought of the letters I'd found in the book in the estate's library, the one my grandda had written to my grandmother Mary.

"My mother held the entire family together. When she died, it was like the entire family died with her. The day after her wake, Da sent me to a boarding school and never wrote me a single letter."

"Like father, like son?" I couldn't help but point out.

Da guffawed. "Touché. But your grandda was a real piece of shite. Never cared for anybody except my mother—not even his only son. But theirs was a grand romance, you know. She was from a well-to-do, upper-crust family who disowned her when she ran off with Da. Just like I did with your mam, actually. Like father, like son, once again."

Da began to skim his finger along the edge of the clock. "Da bought this for Mam when they married. It reminded her of home." He pointed to the flowers that were delicately painted on the clock face. "Do you recognize these?"

"No."

"They're red carnations. They're the flower of the Salasian royal family." Da's eyes locked with mine. "Your grandmother, my mother, was a princess of Salasia."

You know the feeling when you're at the top of a rollercoaster, the moment right before it plunges down to the ground? That was what my stomach felt like in that moment. Like everything I'd ever believed had been turned upside down, topsy turvy, a merry-go-round that I'd never wanted to ride in the first place.

"Princess Mary was the daughter of Prince Jean, younger sister of Prince Louis." Da got up and went to a rickety bookshelf in the corner of his apartment, pulling out a large book. He flipped through the pages and opened it to a family tree. "Your grandmother, Princess Mary. Here. And Prince Louis' son is the current Sovereign Prince of Salasia, Etienne…"

I followed his finger. Below Prince Etienne was a name I knew well: Prince Olivier. To the right was my father's name and then Liam's and my name.

"I don't understand," I said in a rush. "Are Olivier and I…?"

Da started laughing, so hard that he began to cough. It took a few moments for his voice to return, which made the anticipation all the worse. "You'd be second cousins, but considering he's most likely a bastard, it seems as though you two are not, in fact, related." Da's eyebrows rose to his hairline. "Are you going to faint? Should I find some smelling salts?"

His amused tone just made my brain fog dissipate more quickly. As I took in this information, I realized that it could change everything.

If Prince Olivier wasn't the true heir to the Salasian throne, then who was?

"Are you a prince, then?" I said.

"Not in name, not since the royal family stripped my mam of her title. But now they're in a bit of a bind, hmm?" Da leaned back in the couch cushions. "If it were to become public knowledge that Olivier is a bastard, then I would be next in line. Unless Olivier's father is able to produce a legitimate child, although

Princess Alexandra is now too old. And divorce isn't an option, either. Of course, he could always act like Henry VIII and have her beheaded."

I didn't laugh at the joke.

"What do you want? The crown?" I said.

"God, no. Besides, my lass, I'm dying." At my stare, he shrugged. "Lung cancer. I guess that's what happens when you smoke cigarettes most of your life. No, I don't have much time left. But I would like my time to be comfortable, if that's what you're asking."

If Da were the next legitimate heir, that would mean when he died, Liam, my brother, would be next in line as the eldest. Then me. Me, Niamh Gallagher, a girl who'd just wanted to find her father and who'd stumbled upon secrets she'd never thought possible.

And then I thought about Olivier. He was alone. He'd be devastated at reading those letters. His entire life would be ruined; he'd lose everything he'd been brought up to believe was his birthright. All because of something his mother—and perhaps his adopted father —had done.

"The thing is, I'll go to the press with this information if the Royal Family doesn't meet my demands." Da said the words casually. "And if I do that, that means your brother would eventually become the Hereditary Prince of Salasia."

I stood up. "I need to go. I need to find Olivier."

"Yes, yes, find your lover boy. Go comfort him. I'm sure he's quite distraught."

I stared at him, incredulous. "Do you know why I wanted to find you?" My voice was hoarse. "I wanted to find you because I wanted to believe there was some reason, something I couldn't possibly know, as to why you left Mam and Liam and me. I hoped you would've become someone better, that you'd regret what you'd done. But I don't think you regret anything, do you?"

I squared my shoulders, refusing to let him see me cry. "I expected better of you than you ever expected of yourself. And after I leave here, I never want to speak to you again. You were dead to me when I was a child, and now as an adult, you're still dead and gone. Goodbye, Connor Gallagher. May God have mercy on your soul."

Da's expression didn't change. He didn't say good-bye. He merely lit another cigarette and said as I opened the door, "Be sure to lock it behind you. That's a good girl."

CHAPTER TWENTY

C ara met me in at the entrance to the estate before I'd even toed off my shoes. "Ma'am, Mr. Valady wants to speak with you immediately in the library."

I grimaced. "Thanks, Cara. I was going to go search for him anyway. When did he arrive back here? Do you know?"

"He arrived before you left for your appointment, I believe."

So he'd made a point to avoid me. Great. "Oh, well. We must've missed each other." I turned to go upstairs, but I looked over my shoulder to add, "Can you bring up coffee and snacks in, say, an hour? We'll probably need it."

"Of course." She bobbed a curtsy and hurried off. Despite my best efforts to tell all the employees here that they absolutely did not need to bow and curtsy, habits died hard. Olivier had seemed to instantly feel comfortable with the show of deference. He'd make a better owner of this grand estate than I would, that was for sure.

I walked up the stairs slowly. My body felt heavy, like all of the revelations had physically weighed it down. My heart thumped loudly in my ears.

Da might've been wrong about Olivier. The letters could be someone else's.

I told myself that, but my gut wasn't convinced.

When I opened the door to the library, it took me a moment to find Olivier. He was sitting in a chair in front of one of the bay windows, simply staring into the distance. He looked up when he heard me approach, but he didn't rise. He just steepled his fingers.

Where did anyone begin? I opened my mouth, but Olivier beat me to it.

"I'm assuming, based on your expression, that your father told you everything," he said quietly.

I watched as a gull soared across the wide ocean. I suddenly wished I were out there, away from the stress of this tete-a-tete. I could practically feel the tension vibrating off of Olivier.

"If you're referring to the letters," I said slowly, "then yes. He showed them to me. That being said, they don't necessarily prove anything."

Olivier's knuckles turned white. "I appreciate your optimism, but they're exactly what they seem. They prove that, more than likely, I'm a bastard."

I flinched. Olivier, though, was pure stone. His face was blank. I could only tell he was feeling anything by the way he flexed his fingers in a distinct rhythm.

I sat across from him. "Those letters could be forgeries. They could be from other people. You don't know for sure—"

"You're sweet, Niamh." His tone was almost condescending. "But it puts all the pieces together, pieces I've always wondered about. Why I look nothing like my father, and very little like my mother, either. Why my parents are so distant with each other. And why my mother was desperate for me to find this clock. It wasn't about the clock at all: it was about what was hidden inside."

Olivier's gaze caught mine. He smiled, but there was no joy in it. "It makes sense, when I think of so many parts of my childhood that were strange. In a way, I'm relieved to have confirmation."

"I don't believe you. You can't be this calm about this. Your entire life, everything you've been raised to believe, it's over. Or potentially over."

"I'm calm because any other emotion is a waste of time."

I wanted to shake him. I wanted him to yell, scream, cry. I wanted him to act like a human being. Instead, he retained that princely distance, the same icy arrogance that had made me dislike him when we'd first met.

"Emotion isn't a waste of time. Jesus Christ. I'm devastated for you." I took his hands, and I tried to warm up his fingers. "My heart breaks for you, and for your father, your mother. Did your father know? Or is he still in the dark? And what about your mom? Was she in love with this other man but she had to marry your father?"

With every word, I watched a flush crawl up Olivier's face. He pulled his hand away from mine and slowly got up. Leaning over the window ledge, he gripped the dark wood, his head bowed.

"My mother—if one can even call her that—has kept my true parentage a secret my entire life." His voice was strained. "I have been living a lie for twenty-five years, because of her." He turned to face me. The scorn in his expression made me rear backward. "I don't feel any pity for her. She made her own bed when she slept with another man and tried to pass off the child as my father's."

I got up, not wanting Olivier to loom over me like some terrifying specter. "You're angry now, but once you speak with her——"

"I never want to see her again," he snarled, so harshly that it felt almost like a physical blow.

"Olivier..." I tried to touch him. I tried to hug him, but he rebuffed me.

"Stop. Please, for the love of God. I don't want your pity. That look on your face? 'Poor little prince. What will he do now?'"

"I'm not pitying you. I'm trying to be supportive."

"I don't want your support. You, your father—you've done enough. I don't need any of this, and I don't need you to hold my hand and tell me it'll all be just fine, when you and I both know it won't be. It's over. It's all fucking *over*."

I felt angry tears press behind my lids. I could read between the lines: we were over, too.

"You have to know that I had no idea about any of this," I said. "My da was behind this. He's the one trying to extort money out of your family, not me."

"I'm aware. But at the end of day, you're still the daughter of the man who could ruin my life, and my father's, within a moment's notice. You have more to gain from this than anyone, besides your father."

"How dare you." I stepped closer to him, barely restraining myself from shaking him. "How dare you accuse me of trying to gain from all of this. I never wanted this to happen. I wanted to find my da, not have this royal family baby daddy drama fuck everything up! I never wanted a cent from my da, and I definitely don't want a cent from your family, either."

Olivier's expression was so cold, so distant, that it was like a knife to my heart. "Then I suppose this is goodbye. I've already booked a flight back to Salasia."

Now the tears couldn't be held back. My bottom lip trembled. I wiped the tears away and raised my chin. "Goodbye, then."

Olivier held out his hand. After a long moment, I took it. He raised it to his lips and kissed the back of it.

By that evening, he was gone.

CHAPTER TWENTY-ONE

I spent the next two weeks at the estate. I spent a lot of time in bed and the rest of the time either in the library or wandering along the beach.

One day I went to the spot where I'd first met Olivier when he'd been playing gardener, but the plants in question had been moved elsewhere. It was just as well. I didn't need any more reminders that he existed.

"He sounds like a bloody idiot," Liam had said to me multiple times now. "Not worth your time. He can go rot."

Mari, Liam's wife, had taken a more measured approach. "It sounds like he cares for you, and he was clearly in shock. Plus, if what your dad said is true…" She'd given Liam That Look, and he'd just grunted.

Liam hadn't been overly thrilled with the news of our sharing DNA with the Salasian royal family. He'd at first said that Da had just been spinning tales to mess with everyone. But when I did some more research here at the estate, I discovered that Da hadn't been pulling our legs at all.

Da was the cousin of the current reigning prince, Olivier's father. Well, his adoptive father. As far as Olivier's parentage, that was apparently still murky.

Liam, being the ever so helpful big brother, had ribbed me hard for kissing my almost-cousin. "Never took you for a girl like that," he'd said as he'd laughed at me.

"We're not cousins! I keep telling you that!"

"Doesn't make it any less hilarious, baby sister."

"Besides, even if we were related, we're second cousins. It's not that bad."

Okay, it would've been pretty awkward. This wasn't the nineteenth century where marrying your cousin—or having a serious make-out with some cunnilingus with one—was kosher.

Most of all, Liam had urged me to come back home. "There's nothing there for you now. Da isn't going to change. Your prince is gone. Come back to Seattle and we'll figure things out."

I was tempted. I wanted to go home; I wanted to use ugly American dollars and to go to a grocery store that had one entire aisle dedicated to cereals. I wanted to accidentally make eye contact with a fellow Seattleite and then awkwardly look away, acting like it'd never happened. I even wanted to go to Pike Place Market during the summer and get mowed down by tourists as they almost got hit in the face with a giant, flying fish.

But I had unfinished business. Namely, I'd never told Olivier about Da being the heir to the throne. I'd called Olivier and had texted him too many times to count. I'd left him cajoling voicemails. I'd sent him frustrated texts. The seemingly millionth time I'd tried contacting him, the number had come back as disconnected.

He'd fucking blocked me. I couldn't believe it. After everything that had happened, he had the audacity to ignore me.

I didn't stop to think that flying to Salasia would be a bad idea. I'd bought the ticket before I'd let myself have second thoughts. On the flight, I pondered how I'd even get Olivier to speak with me. Did I just storm into the castle—did they live in a castle? or a palace?—and demand that he talk to me?

Instead, I stalked social media. I figured out where Olivier's favorite cafes, restaurants, and bars were. It didn't take long before I discovered that he would buy a cappuccino every morning from a cafe that overlooked the Mediterranean Ocean. Sometimes another person got it for him. But on Sundays, he bought it himself.

The locals were used to him, for the most part. Sitting outside of the cafe, the smell of the sea and of fresh coffee in the air, I waited for him to exit. He wore a ball cap this time, so I guessed he didn't want to be recognized. But I'd recognize him anywhere.

As he walked to his car—he'd driven himself—I headed straight for him. "Olivier!" I yelled. I took off my sunglasses so he could get a good look at my angry face.

He swiveled toward the sound of my voice. His eyes widened, but then he just sipped his cappuccino as he looked down his nose at me.

"You found me," he said, too pleasantly.

"Shouldn't you have a bodyguard? I could kill you right now."

He sipped his coffee. "Well? Are you here to assassinate me?"

I scowled. "No. I just wanted to talk." I crossed my arms. "You wouldn't answer my calls."

Sighing, he went to open the passenger door. "Get in. We'll talk at home."

~

HOME, of course, meant Salasia Palace. I had to keep my jaw from dropping as Olivier took me to his office within the palace's walls. The walls were draped with gilding and artwork, the halls alone so huge that you could've fit a thousand people in them.

A few servants gave us strange looks, but for the most part, they were too well-trained to wonder why some girl wearing dirty Converse was following the prince to his office.

Olivier gestured at me to sit before sitting behind his desk. The room itself was almost cozy compared to the rest of the palace. The window behind Olivier had a view of the capital, the sky a beautiful, bright blue. The room itself smelled like leather and expensive things. I perched on the edge of my chair, afraid to touch anything.

"I have something to tell you," I said. I swallowed. "I meant to tell you that day you left, and that's why I've been annoying about talking to you."

Olivier leaned back in his chair. "Would this have anything to do with your father's claim to the throne?"

"You know? How? When?" My voice rose with each word. "Why the hell would you block my number with something this important to talk about!"

"I blocked your number because you wouldn't take

no for an answer. I was going to speak with you—on my own time. But I should've known you'd come to Salasia and spring yourself upon me. That's more your style."

"I mean, I prefer a quick phone call than spending money on a plane ticket."

His lips twitched slightly. That sparkle in his eyes that had so captivated me returned, but just for a quick second. Then it was gone again.

"Your father, when I went to collect the clock, told me the great news. He showed me the family tree. I'd heard of my great aunt Mary, of course, but all I'd ever known was that she'd run off with someone unsuitable and that there was no reason to speak of her. Then she'd die fairly young. Apparently, she'd kept a low enough profile that the family hadn't known she'd had a son." He folded his hands. "Or perhaps she didn't want them to know."

"Okay, so you know. And if you're really a bastard…"

He let the question hang in the air. Then, all he said was, "Yes, it's true."

"So, what happens? I mean, I know your secret, and so does my da. But my da is dying, and I know Liam won't want anything to do with this life. So as long as no one knows, you can keep being the prince."

I felt silly then, coming all this way to tell Olivier something he already knew. I should've just found his Facebook and messaged him. (Did royals have their own Facebook? Probably not.)

"I would agree with you," said Olivier, "but your beloved father isn't inclined to play so nicely. You see, his threats to reveal this information to the press are increasing, because my family isn't interested in paying him the exorbitant amount of money he's demanding. So, I suppose we're at a bit of a stalemate."

"Oh. Shit. I'm sorry. But you said my da gave you the clock?"

"Yes, but he made copies of the letters, so it hardly mattered who possessed it."

I picked at a stray thread on my jeans. Then Olivier rose from his chair and stood over me. He leaned against his desk.

"There is another solution to this problem," he said.

With the sun shining behind him, he looked like some golden god. I felt my body heat, remembering our one night together. One side of his delicious mouth lifted, like he knew what I was thinking about.

"The only solution I can think of is breaking my da's kneecaps," I joked.

"Nothing that violent. No, you see, you can be the one to make this right."

I blinked. "Me? How?"

"Although your brother, being the eldest, would be the heir, as you said, the last thing he'd want to do is uproot his family's life to become the Sovereign Prince of Salasia one day. And I most certainly do not want to give this crown to someone who would despise it."

"I'm still not following, sorry."

He shook his head. Then, caging me in with his arms, his face uncomfortably close, he said, "You would be next in line to the throne if your brother were to abdicate. Which he most certainly would."

His breath was hot against my face. I felt like a rabbit caught in the gaze of a cobra.

"So in exchange for making this right, for not completely upending your beloved brother's life, here is the solution to both of our problems: become a princess of Salasia in both name and by blood."

"How?" My voice was barely a whisper.

He paused then went for the kill. "By marrying me."

ABOUT THE AUTHOR

A coffee addict and cat lover, Iris Morland writes sexy and funny contemporary romances. If she's not reading or writing, she enjoys binging on Netflix shows and cooking something delicious.